The Disappearance Of Timothy Dawson

NATHAN PARKER

ISBN-13: 978-1982078720

ISBN-10: 1982078723

NADINA AND SONNY

A thousand books couldn't describe the love I have for you. Thank you for making life so full of joy.

MUM AND DAD

Thank you for your constant, selfless faith and support. I would not be who I am today without you.

ACKNOWLEDGMENTS

Thank you to those I love for the inspiration and encouragement to keep going.

They say everybody has a book within them; you just need to search inside your soul and put the words on a page. Thank you to my brother, as without our lessons in life, I would not have been able to write this book. I am proud of the man and Brother you have become.

Thank you to my proof readers, for entertaining my endless requests to read and reread. Your feedback and enthusiasm has spurred me on to the finish line.

Thank you to Andrew Ray for helping me to create the cover and to Mike Vettese for the wonderful photograph.

Thank you finally to Nadina, for getting excited with me, listening to my ideas, sharing my frustrations and allowing me to have my head in my laptop for the past year or so.

CHAPTER ONE

"Pay the money you owe, or you will regret ever being in my debt!"

The voice from downstairs was growing louder and more intimidating. What started out as a knock at the door and a muffled exchange had now escalated into a threatening argument. The voice was male, as the visitors collecting money or dropping off 'packages' often were at his house.

Tommy lay on his bed contemplating going down to his mum's aid. It wasn't the first time he'd heard these kinds of threats from the unsavoury characters who so frequently paid his mum and brother a visit. He tried not to get involved in their affairs where possible.

"Just one more day, please!" Tommy heard his mum plead, "I promise I'll have it for you," she said with a noticeable slur.

Drunk, again. The fire within him to protect his mum had faded some time ago, when he realised she had no interest in protecting him. It was still there, just, a flicker perhaps, but the blazing furnace present in most children to protect the person who gave them life, just wasn't as apparent anymore.

Tommy heard the clatter of the door and a fumble – it sounded like the man was forcing his way in. He had to act. *For fuck sake, here we go again,* he thought. He jumped up from his bed and out onto the landing. The landing to his home was bare. Bare walls with chipped plaster and brick work peeking through, bare floorboards, bare of any life or care whatsoever and the theme ran through the whole house. He made his way down the stairs until he reached half way and could see the scene in front of him.

A man in his early forties wearing a black bomber jacket, had his mum, Theresa, pinned up against the open front door. Tommy felt the cold October breeze as it blustered into the house and up the stairs. The house was cold at the best of times let alone with the door wide open. It was dark, but Tommy saw that the man had a shaven head, probably out of necessity rather than choice as his head seemed far shinier on the top than it did the sides. He had a gaunt face and profound cheekbones, a goatee beard and a tattoo of a smiley face on his neck behind his ear – the unmistakable symbol of Smiler's crew.

Tommy saw the tattoo and had to compose himself. *Shit! He works for Smiler*. He'd heard about the tattoo and what – or rather who – it represented. He recalled stories about Smiler and his gang of thugs.

People would whisper and share folk tales about his criminal empire, about how he had people killed at the click of his fingers not before torturing them first, rumours about how he manipulated and controlled everyone he encountered and about how his minions had to have a tattoo to prove their commitment to him. The more street wise kids would talk and gloat, in an attempt to build kudos, about how Smiler controlled everything in Granville's gangland, including the seedy underworld of heroin and crack distribution. Tommy would distance himself from the hearsay, but always listened with an interested and concerned ear, as that was the very world that his mum and brother dipped in and out of all too often.

Smiler was thought of as an urban myth by those who were fortunate to have never encountered him, but Tommy knew that in the darkest of hours, even an atheist can become a believer. Smiler was a 21st century bogeyman and unfortunately, those who had been sucked in by the drugs, the intimidation and the broken promises, knew all too well how very real he was. Very few knew Smiler's actual name or what he looked like, but everybody in Granville knew his alias.

The man, who now stood inside the doorway to his home, was armed with a license to torment and terrorise, a license that the iconic Smiley face tattoo provided and everybody in Granville knew it. He looked threatening and almost aroused as he seemed to be relishing the position he found himself in, his tongue ever so slightly out of his mouth and caressing his top lip.

"Oi!" Tommy yelled, masking his nerves with enough conviction to get the man's attention and break him from his perverse trance, "You heard her, she said she'll pay you tomorrow – now piss off before I call the Police!"

The man sniggered as he looked around the house in disgust, easing his grip on his mum ever so slightly, "You lot haven't even got a phone, you bunch of peasants."

Tommy was used to people judging him and his family and actually, he didn't usually blame them. He had learnt to use insults and judgements to make him stronger and more determined to break free from the shackles of poverty and adversity by which he was bound. This time however, Tommy wasn't taking it from a woman-beating drug pusher.

Tommy waved his battered, old mobile phone in his hand – the man didn't need to know he had no credit to call anyone. Tommy recalled an assembly at school in which they learned that an emergency call was free anyway, in case the man called his bluff.

The man assessed his situation reluctantly. He looked torn between his pride and the thought that his boss would be really upset with him if he had an altercation with the Police whilst on the clock. Tommy watched on uneasily as, grudgingly, the man with the goatee beard conceded. He threw his mum to the ground at the foot of the stairs and stepped out of the house.

"Tomorrow at noon... or else!" he warned, pointing his finger aggressively, before storming off and disappearing into the night.

Tommy made his way down the last few stairs and helped his mum to her feet. She was drunk; he could smell the alcohol from her breath which had formed an unpleasant stench mixed with the smell of cigarettes and tooth decay.

"No need to ask what he wanted then?" Tommy remarked, as he assisted his mum into the living room and onto the couch.

She reached for her cigarettes. Despite learning not to ask too many questions when it came to the delivery of goods and the collection of money, the once small, scared boy that used to creep around the house not wanting to upset the chaotic status quo had been forced to grow up and so Tommy was now rarely afraid to say what was on his mind.

"Oh that's great Tommy, you think you're so bleeding clever don't you, go ahead and make your stupid, sarcastic remarks!" Theresa scorned. She was upset, lashing out towards others, which Tommy had become accustomed to.

"Where's Derek? I'm pretty sure, as my older brother and part of the pair who are actually involved in this mess, it should be him shooing away debt collectors, or whoever the hell that was, not me?" Tommy asked rhetorically, brushing off Theresa attack, knowing full well his brother would be passed out in his room, or any other random room in town for that matter, after his latest hit of heroin.

Tommy was actually surprised his mum was still remotely upright, given that it was after 7pm. Mum and Derek shared the same interests – mainly drink and drugs – and were usually flat out on another planet by now, the reality of life too grim to face and the warm, comfort blanket that heroin provided too much of a temptation to resist.

"Don't be like that Thomas, he's been upset today!" Theresa snapped defensively. Her efforts at appearing sensitive were feeble, as she tried to place a cigarette in her mouth, her trembling hands clearly making that task a little trickier than it should be. "He struggles this time of year, it's around the time of your dad leaving us," she said, with a look of disdain, "he still finds it tough. I keep telling him we're better off without him, but will he listen? Will he 'eck!"

Tommy could see through Theresa's attempt to excuse Derek's behaviour. A stranger may have seen or heard a mother's instinct, defending and protecting her eldest son from Tommy's quips; however Tommy knew the truth. It was to justify her own irresponsible behaviour rather than to protect Derek; he'd seen and heard it a million times. She spent a lot of her time wallowing in the past, sometimes fondly, often bitter, always under the influence of drink, drugs or both.

Tommy rolled his eyes. He had no idea it was close to the anniversary of his dad leaving them, he was only two years old when he left. He'd asked his mum about him in the past but she was always very vague, defensive and unpleasant whenever the subject came up, so in the interest of peace, he stopped asking. He knew nothing about him, or why he left. He was starting to assume he'd had enough of his mum though; she was enough to drive any sane person away. Tommy was sure his dad had his reasons for leaving, he had always felt quite neutrally about it - in this case, ignorance was bliss.

"So that's this week's excuse for you two is it – dad?" Tommy teased. He didn't live with as much fear anymore. No longer as frightened to upset his unstable and volatile mother, he pitied her more often than anything else. "Last week it was because they hadn't paid you the right benefits so you couldn't possibly face the world, the week before it was because the man at the job centre had looked at Derek funny… yeah right, it took you 6 months to get over the local MP getting elected in again – you didn't even vote, you don't even know anything about politics!"

"You won't understand, you're just a kid," Theresa said flippantly, as she exhaled a cloud of smoke from her super-king cigarette.

The nicotine did his mum's hair no favours. It was straw like, her fingers and lips were tobacco stained and where once sat a pretty face and dazzling eyes, now appeared a gaunt expression and dark, sunken eyes filled with regret and resentment.

Despite lack of money, his mum always managed to have a cigarette in her hand, mouth or resting on the grooves of her ashtray, which she had clearly 'borrowed' from The Junction pub about 4 years ago. The nicotine was gradually turning the walls from a shade of cream to golden amber.

Tommy hated that phrase - *just a kid*. His mum and brother seemed to use it whenever he gained the upper hand in an argument or discussion, although granted sensible discussions were few and far between at his home, 10 Frampton Road. He didn't hate it because he wanted to be seen as an adult or aspired to do adult things. He hated it because he found it depressingly ironic that his mum and brother referred to him as a kid so frequently, despite him being the one who does their washing, the cleaning, the food shopping - sort of, who puts them to bed when they've passed out from drinking or chasing too much and he's the one who has done all of this whilst maintaining a good enough presence at school to keep the social from knocking at the door all these years. *Just a kid*, he'd say to himself, *now there's a thought*.

He looked around the living room, an empty bottle of vodka cast aside on the dirty carpet, the huge rip in the couch with the once white fluff that had now been exposed that long it was sporting a tinge of yellow, the CD/Cassette player which still was without a story or paper trail as to its origin, an overflowing ashtray on the coffee table and his sneering mother now slumped in the middle of the ripped couch scowling back at him. Despite his bravery and his self-made pretence – or defence rather – he felt a slight sinking in his stomach. He hated all of this; his surroundings, the lack of connection with his mum and her all round bitterness and lack of awareness and responsibility. He sensed it was time to depart before a real argument was ignited.

"Whatever, Mum. I'm going back upstairs to do my coursework."

Tommy took himself upstairs, away from the mess and the chaos, to the only place in the house which remained tidy and clean – his bedroom. This was his space, with a worn Stone Roses poster on the wall, his TV which was small, old and needed a slap round the back from time to time, and his bed, which despite being the same bed and mattress he'd had as long as he could remember, was one of his favourite places.

Tommy laid on his bed and fiddled around with his earphones, attempting to untangle them ready to listen to some music. He loved music and had a varied taste. It was his escape, his escape within his 7'x10' haven of tranquillity. He popped an earphone in each ear and hit play on his second hand MP3 player.

Tommy tried to forget about the incident which had just occurred; he started to think about escaping and becoming more than just another fallen statistic of Granville. In his room he felt as safe and relaxed as a 16 year old boy could feel, living with two heroin addicts and wondering when drug dealers will next come and boot the door down demanding payment – but he wanted more, so much more. Whilst his birth certificate said 16, he knew that his life experiences put him way beyond that. He sat thinking about what life would have been like if he hadn't been blessed with his inner determination and resourcefulness. He wondered what life would have been like if he'd instead followed blindly in his brother's footsteps.

Despite his dismissive and sarcastic remarks to his mum about his brother, Tommy often reflected fondly on a time when he idolised Derek. He had always thought his brother was popular and cool on the surface, but little was known about the inner turmoil which his brother was experiencing in not having a Father or a role model. He now realised that Derek struggled adjusting and without any guidance during his teenage years, he had slipped into the world of drugs to escape reality and cope with his feelings. Unlike himself, he realised that Derek found it extremely difficult not having a Father. Derek was 9 years old when their dad, Timothy, left and the loss seemed to affect him more than Tommy could comprehend. He didn't blame his brother as much anymore for his lifestyle choices, although they frustrated the hell out of him from time to time.

Tommy tried not to live his life focussing on negative stuff like his mum and Derek seemed to do. Whilst they twisted themselves up in knots about how unfair the world was, he was more concerned with escaping this way of life, he dreamed of university or travelling the world and, perhaps more humbling, a family home of his own, bursting with love and affection. He let his mind run away from him, until the harsh reality of who he was and where he lived soon brought him crashing down.

"Thomas!" His mum cried, drowning out his music.

"One minute!" Tommy grumbled, as he climbed off his bed to re-enter the fray. He made his way back downstairs to the lounge.

"Be a diamond and nip to the shop for me love, we're out of milk... and get some tin foil as well whilst you're there." His mum asked. There was a pause and a moment of discomfort, "You know I like to cover the grill tray for the bacon so we don't have to wash it."

Theresa's bitter tongue and scornful tone had diminished and she'd temporarily removed the enormous chip from her shoulder to coincide with her request. *Convenient*, Tommy thought. Tommy also knew the foil wasn't for bacon. He knew because he couldn't remember the last time he'd tasted bacon at home, or the last time his mum cooked in fact. Bacon was a treat in his house and lately, he found that treats were hard to come by. *Least she'll be peaceful tonight*, he thought, *she always seems so peaceful afterwards*. It was a bittersweet feeling for Tommy.

He took the money from his mum, which she scraped together with some silver coins. Buoyed at the prospect of fresh air and a chance to listen to music in peace, Tommy put on his jacket and headed for the door. Track selection: 'To Be Someone' by The Jam.

Tommy day dreamed as he strode down Frampton Road towards Wood Street. *To be someone must be a wonderful thing*. Paul Weller knew the score. He looked out across the dark autumn sky, a thin layer of orange sunlight just falling into the sea. Frampton Road was about a mile inland. It was a steep street, a tunnel of terraced houses almost, which during the day allowed Tommy a perfect viewpoint of the not too distant seafront of Granville. Tonight, he could just about make out the promenade and rollercoasters that the once glorious seaside town was famous for, only these days the once joyful screams of youth had been replaced with the screams of nightmares as a second generation fell into a black hole of poverty, deprivation, drugs and alcohol.

Tommy hated walking down the near the promenade and its back streets and avoided it where he could. He knew kids who gravitated towards there for the tacky amusements and arcades, despite its well known risk of being a magnet for predators and exploitation. It was a place to hang out, find mischief and access an array of illegal activity, with people who wouldn't tell them any different, but Tommy knew that to go down there was just asking for trouble.

He'd often hear old people say the town isn't what it used to be and that made him quite sad. They'd be referring to the hustle and bustle of its once thriving tourism industry which had won the hearts of the whole nation. Now, the only national attention Tommy heard about was it being one of the most disadvantaged areas in the country. *I need to get out of this town,* he thought, as he turned his eyes away from the distant fairground and turned onto Wood Street.

Tommy bought the milk and foil from the shop and began the short distance back home. He popped his earphones back in and away he went. His earphones were black and worn, the small Sony print had rubbed off and he struggled to tell the left from the right, meaning they often slipped out of his ears. This was hardly surprising though, he did have rather sizable ears stuck onto the side of his subtly handsome face, or so people said.

His earphones crackled a little due to a loose connection but he didn't care, *crackly music was better than no music*. Most lads at school had headphones which were really new and cool. Tommy was envious. Yet again it was just another area where he fell short and had to settle for second best, or rather, second hand.

CHAPTER TWO

The following day at school, Tommy met up with his best friend, Kirsten Cole, at break time. He found school tough, not necessarily academically, more socially and finding his place, but his friendship with Kirsten was certainly a ray of sunshine in the jungle that was Wellington Road High School.

"Hey Tommy," Kirsten said with her beaming smile, looking up at him as he approached.

Tommy smiled back and nodded, "Your hair looks good!"

Kirsten's hair was black in colour with dashes of dyed blonde, which she often wore down and wavy. Today he noticed she had it tied up into a hive of curly ringlets and it suited her, it made her face look pretty.

"Ah thanks!" Kirsten said, blushing a little. "Sorry I missed your call last night, my mum needed me to babysit my little sister and she was being a right little nuisance. By the time I'd got her down to bed and done my school work it was past 11 – everything ok?" she asked as they walked across the gravel yard, towards the block where their next lesson was – English Literature.

“Ah don’t worry Kirst, I was just ringing to ask about this English coursework, it’s doing my head in – Shakespeare man, it’s like another language!” Tommy replied.

He knew he was capable and usually got frustrated by his shortcomings. He didn’t feel comfortable sharing this with many people, but Kirsten was somebody he could count on, as had been proven time and time again. He was fully aware that he trusted very few people in his life, but Kirsten certainly made the cut.

“Oh so I’m your tutor now am I?” Kirsten joked, “Not, ‘oh Kirsten I was calling to see how you are’ then?”

They both laughed as Tommy pushed open the blue double doors, the gateway to the English department.

“So I take it you’ve not done it?”

“No, I had a go, just couldn’t get my head around it. Had the perfect evening for it as well, my mum was off her head and out for the count and I’ve no idea where that dope of a brother of mine was...” Tommy said.

Kirsten offered an awkward but supportive smile and Tommy sensed he might have overshared. Kirsten bumped into him with an affectionate nudge to his shoulder.

“I’m sure Mr B. will let you off and give you an extension, he’s pretty cool is Mr B.” she said with a burst of optimism as they approached Mr Bishop’s classroom. Tommy saw the sparkle in Kirsten's eyes and it gave him a little reassurance.

Other than Mr Bishop, a tall, gangly man with a friendly smile and known affectionately as Mr B. by many of the students, Tommy found that he frustrated most teachers. They would say he was bright sure, but that he didn't always apply himself or some other teacher type talk and they would always finish it with their favourite line about unfulfilled potential to really hammer home their disappointment. Mr B. was different; he always tried to help him and seemed to accept him for who he was.

Tommy was desperate to succeed inside, but if a guy like him got attention in class, it meant he got the backlash of the bullies and the gossips, something that he didn't particularly like all that well - although he wasn't shy in defending himself most of the time. Plus, he didn't truly believe he'd ever make it out of Granville, despite his deepest desires, so he was always mindful of false hope, which he felt he acquired with every good grade he received. It was a strange and conflicting balancing act that he often got wrong.

Aside from Kirsten, Tommy saw himself as a bit of a lone wolf and, despite being liked by most, not many people, other than Kirsten, could tell you his intimate details; what he liked, what he didn't, who he was attracted to at school etc. and Tommy liked it that way. He took advantage of the mystique that surrounded him; it meant he never had to drop his guard for anyone.

He enjoyed the fact that his peers found him a bit of a mystery, partly due to him isolating himself from most social groups – he didn't feel like a loner, he just didn't let people in too close. He liked to keep himself to himself; he had no affiliation with the football team, or the break dancers and wannabe M.C.'s, or the smokers behind the bike shed playing 'pitch and toss' with their dinner money, or even, and perhaps less surprisingly, the chess club, who frantically paced between lessons to avoid contact with anyone *outside* of the chess club.

One thing Tommy couldn't do anything about though was everyone knowing about his mum and brother's drug habits. As with every high school, there was a group of loud mouths who took pleasure in making life difficult for some people. It felt to Tommy like Wellington Road High School's band of bullies, led by Craig Hargreaves, seemed to joyfully prey on him and his vulnerabilities whenever they surfaced, creating a constant, exhausting battle that he was just about sick of.

He took his seat over on the far side of the room and got out his pen and English folder; Kirsten sat to the left of him a couple of rows in front. Tommy could still smell the paint from the walls after it was recently decorated with a trio of blue colours, which was apparently good for brain stimulation and creativity.

Mr Bishop took pride in his classroom and had come in over the weekend to paint it himself, that was the kind of guy he was and Tommy respected that. The school was crumbling around them but Mr B. showed defiance and pride, giving up his own time to revitalise his own little corner of Wellington High School.

The lesson got underway and it wasn't long before, sure enough, the Shakespeare coursework was brought up in the discussion and when Tommy was the only one in the class who didn't produce the assignment they were tasked with, he knew what would come next. *Here we go*.

"Please see me at the end of the lesson Mr Dawson." Mr Bishop was blunt and to the point. The "oohs" and "ahhs" rang around the classroom and he felt the burn of the spotlight on him.

"You'd be better writing an essay about a book by William Smack-gear Dawson!" Hargreaves heckled from the back of the class, much to the delight of his cronies, who giggled profusely, "Hey lads, his mum could play Juliet and she could ask Smiler to play Romeo when she goes to pick up her next fix!"

Hargreaves barely finished his sentence before roaring with laughter, proud at how witty he thought he was. Tommy was pissed off; Hargreaves never missed an opportunity to pounce. *How's he turned that one into an insult about my family!*

"Shut it Craig!" snapped Kirsten feistily, before Tommy could even think of a response.

"Ooh, I didn't know Dawson needed his girlfriend to fight his battles for him," said Hargreaves, with a snigger and a high five to his friend, Alex Ingol, who seemed to be stitched to his side wherever they went. Hargreaves' rat-like features were creasing with enjoyment.

Tommy could feel himself burn up, his cheeks turning flush with embarrassment and a little rage too. Thinking it best to simmer down and let it blow over, regardless of how much he felt like striking out at Hargreaves, he began to count in his head. *1, 2, 3...*

Mr B. interjected and settled the class back down, giving Craig Hargreaves a warning in the process. The lesson continued until the bell went, Mr B. dismissed everybody and Tommy stayed behind as requested. He heard Hargreaves and his pals mocking him on the way out and it stung his pride.

"Thomas, what can I do to help?" Mr B. opened up with in his usual reassuring tone, looking up over his glasses, which were perched right on the end of his rather large nose. He had kind eyes with a tiredness that matched the patterned sweater vest he wore so regularly.

"Are you not going to tell me off?" Tommy quizzed.

"Tell you off? Why on earth would I do that?" Mr B. said with a wry smile, "Oh you mean that? That was just so that the class thought I would be giving you a talking to for missing your deadline... I can't be having them getting any ideas!" He laughed, "Thomas, I'm here to help, will an extension suffice? Or do you need a little more tuition?"

Tommy was pleased with Mr B.'s supportive gesture; he felt warmth and belief from him, something that other teachers lacked.

"Some help and an extension would be good to be honest Mr B.?" Tommy chanced.

"Tommy, you're a very capable student and a young man with superb potential... I know you have difficulties going on, I mean, school is probably the least of your worries and I'm not saying that to pry.

Speaking truthfully, I think half the students in this school have difficulties going on. However difficult you find it to apply yourself in school; this place is your ticket out of Granville, you just need to decide if you really want it." Mr B. paused for a second as Tommy pondered. "Look, all I'm saying is, if you need help, you just need to ask."

They had a chat and Tommy left with an extension of one week and feeling reassured about the Shakespeare assignment, the same couldn't be said about Hargreaves and his band of goons.

Lunch time came and went. Tommy grabbed a bite to eat from the canteen with Kirsten. He was on free school dinners and he'd always offer Kirsten his cookie. Deep down, he had kind and considerate tendencies but he tried to keep them to a minimum at school with subtle gestures such as this, not wanting to attract any unwanted attention from the circling vultures. Kirsten smiled, as she always did when he did stuff like this, saying it was cute or whatever. It felt strange when she said those kinds of things, but the feeling seemed to be growing on him lately.

One thing that continued to astound him about Kirsten as they grew up, was that she still shied away from attention like she had when they first started school, despite the development of her external beauty. She'd always focussed on being a nice person and she had mastered that in his eyes. He found that she focussed much less on make-up and push up bras than the rest of the girls in his year, which was a relief given that he wouldn't know where to start with a conversation about either of those things.

During lunch they sat with some of the people from Kirsten's form group who Tommy thought were pretty cool to hang out with, no pressure to act up or be something he didn't want to be. No pressure, he liked that, it was refreshing and liberating.

The best thing about lunch time was no Craig Hargreaves. He was probably outside picking fights with some Year 9 boys, or stealing some kid's football. Tommy couldn't stand him. It was still bugging him what happened in Mr Bishop's class earlier.

Hargreaves was everything that Tommy disliked in a person – a spoilt brat. The more Tommy thought about him, the more his image became emblazoned onto the walls of his mind, infuriating him further. His pointy nose, his slicked back hair and his attempt at facial hair that looked like a gust of wind would take it right off.

Tommy found him more annoying than intimidating. He was a bully, plain and simple; he triumphed in other people's misery. Hargreaves was the son of the largest furniture supplier in Granville, Birds Furniture. His dad would always turn up in his flash, black Mercedes car to pick Craig up. The pair of them would smirk at Tommy with an air of arrogance that made him feel paranoid and self-conscious. Tommy always felt Mr Hargreaves stared a little longer than a grown man should at a 16 year old boy; his scowl was piercing and made Tommy uncomfortable.

Tommy hated the fact that he was also a little envious of Craig, after all he had a Dad who, for all his faults, did at least seem interested in him and he always had the latest fashion and gadgets, seemingly making it his mission to demoralise and humiliate anybody who couldn't keep up – especially Tommy.

They'd had their share of scrapes and scuffles in the past, but nowadays Tommy tried to ignore him and get on with his own life – that was until today.

Kirsten was in the classroom next door to Tommy for the last period of the day. He spent the lesson going through the motions; mulling over his beef with Hargreaves, wondering what mess would be waiting for him when he got home and also, rather refreshingly, he thought about Kirsten's hair and how nice it made her look today.

The bell sounded to signal the end of the day and the usual daily rush began. Bags were already whipped up from under desks, coats half put on as the masses of students darted for classroom doors across the school. Tommy met Kirsten on the way out and headed down the science block stairs amidst a wave of eager students destined for freedom. They moved on to the main corridor and past the languages department, where Mrs Veronique stopped them.

"Thomas," she said in her thick French accent, "I meant to pass this on to you; it's your revision book."

Tommy felt uncomfortable. He looked awkwardly at the book and then at Mrs Veronique. She was a short lady, with thin, circular framed glasses, pale skin that was almost translucent in places, a bob hair style with a perfect centre parting and a rather off-putting mono-brow. She spent her days barking at the front of her class and reducing first years to tears.

"Erm, Miss... I can't afford to buy it, I'm sorry." Tommy said with a little tinge of red creeping into his cheeks, which resembled his school tie.

"Ahh, I knew you would say that Thomas," she said with a surprisingly comforting tone, "this book was sent extra from the company you see, so no charge for you or Mum, ok?" Mrs Veronique finished with a subtle wink. Tommy took the book and nodded in appreciation.

"Thanks Miss," Tommy said, gratefully as Mrs Veronique turned to go back into her classroom. He knew that she had paid for his book. He was embarrassed but humbled by her surprising kindness. Two favours off two teachers in one day. *Maybe today was turning out to be a pretty good day after all.*

"I love her accent," said Kirsten, "It's so French!" She laughed as they continued towards the Block B exit at the side of school to head home.

The delay with Mrs Veronique had meant the school was quiet now. They were just passing Mr Turner's office, the Head Teacher, when they were faced with a situation they could have done without. Hargreaves.

"What you been doing Dawson, creeping round some more teachers? 'Ooh my names Tommy Dawson and I'm so poor that teachers feel sorry for me'," he mocked.

Laughter erupted from Hargreaves' backing band as their leader churned out another one hit wonder. It didn't ever seem to matter the quality of his insults, he always got a wave of laughter off his disciples.

"Leave off Hargreaves, I can't be arsed with this today," Tommy said, attempting diplomacy for an easy life and a quick exit.

"Hey lads, you heard that, Dawson wants me to leave off! Wonder if that's what your mum said to your dad before he bailed and left you to rot in that smack den you call a home!" He cackled. It was never clear whether he was the kind of bully who was insecure, or the kind of bully who took genuine pleasure in being vindictive.

"I'm warning you Craig, don't push me." Tommy's words were cold. He could feel a bubbling sensation in his gut, adrenalin had kicked in and he'd had enough, but he knew Hargreaves was too obnoxious to take him seriously. This wasn't going to end well.

"Just piss off Hargreaves, leave us alone," Kirsten added.

Hargreaves closed the gap and he and his friends shut off the corridor so Tommy and Kirsten couldn't get past. They were penned in.

"Why what you gonna' do, hey? You tramp!" Hargreaves poked Tommy in the chest as he finished. He was cocky but complacent. As he looked around to admire his small audience, Tommy stuck a firm head butt flush to the bridge of Hargreaves' nose. Crunch.

"Arghhhh!" screamed Hargreaves, but before he could react to what had happened, the office door flew open. The crowd attempted to disperse as Mr Turner stormed out onto the corridor, pink with rage and ready to spit nails at the first person who met his eyes, which unfortunately for Tommy, was him.

Tommy was rooted to the spot as Hargreaves skulked away and made a swift exit down the corridor. To give him a tiny bit of credit, Hargreaves didn't make a fuss or tell Mr Turner what had happened, but due to his bloody nose, it didn't take a genius to figure out.

"In my office, NOW!" Mr Turner bellowed. "You too, Miss Cole!"

Tommy and Kirsten shuffled sheepishly towards Mr Turner's office, avoiding eye contact with their commanding Head Teacher – and each other – at all costs. There was a distant cry of 'you're gonna' pay for this, Dawson!' from way down the corridor which was unmistakably Craig Hargreaves, despite a busted nose.

The threat barely registered with Tommy, who felt he was guilty without trial, walking down the green mile and dragging his best friend along with him. Mr Turner could be a compassionate Head Teacher and usually seemed to prefer praising his students as opposed to punishing them, so his rage, although understandable, was a little out of character and surprising. Then it became clear.

They entered Mr Turner's office and Tommy instantly saw a figure he was unfamiliar with. A tall and imposing man, around sixty years old, Tommy guessed. He wore a sharp, grey, three piece suit, with a gold watch chain burrowing into his waistcoat pocket. He had thinning grey hair and a chubby face, glistening with sweat.

"How dare you cause such mayhem in our corridors, especially when we have such an honourable, special guest visiting!" Mr Turner's voice boomed and filled his rather large and swanky office, which wasn't particularly in keeping with the rest of the school. "You've embarrassed me, the school and Councillor Jim Carruthers here," Mr Turner gestured towards the tall, chubby faced man in the grey suit. "You better start talking Thomas as I'm intrigued to know how Mr Hargreaves ended up with a nose like Henry Cooper!"

Mr Turner had finished his piece, for now, and stood there waiting for an explanation from Tommy. His face was scarlet, his arms folded and his foot tapping impatiently. Cllr Carruthers said nothing, but offered a reassuring look which put Tommy a little more at ease.

"Sir, Hargreaves was giving me loads of stick about my mum and my dad, he had it coming to him, he's horrible to kids in this school and it's about time he got his comeuppance." Tommy pleaded, before realising what he'd said wasn't going to do him any favours with Mr Turner in front of an apparent special visitor.

"Do you call that an explanation Dawson, not even an inkling of an apology – don't even think about it Miss Cole!" Mr Turner snapped seeing Kirsten was itching to defend Tommy. "You are 16 years old Tom," he continued with a more soothing tone, "you need to let children like Craig Hargreaves behave like children and you concentrate on growing up and moving past the playground tittle tattle, however hurtful the remarks can be."

"I know sir, I'm sorry Mr Turner," Tommy conceded. He knew he was right, but Hargreaves just pushed all of his wrong buttons. Mr Turner produced a fake throat clearing cough as he pointed his eyes towards Cllr Carruthers, "And I'm sorry to you too Sir for embarrassing our school like this, it won't happen again." Tommy finished, to the satisfied nod of Mr Turner.

Cllr Jim Carruthers sprang into life, leaving his perch on Mr Turner's large, solid oak desk to slowly move around the room, with a wide smile and an interesting manner. He had Tommy's attention straight away.

"Thomas Dawson? Son of Timothy?" he asked. Tommy was taken aback and simply nodded, unsure where this was going. "Thomas Dawson, do not worry in the slightest my boy, I knew your father, and if I was in your shoes and that young man was insulting me about my father, who I did not know, then I too would have been extremely tempted to, as Mr Turner put it, arrange his nose like Henry Cooper's – sorry Mr Turner, I know that's not the message you were sending to the boy."

Cllr Carruthers spoke as though he was opening up a case in a court of law, striding casually across the room, with his hands together behind his back and talking in a rather unusual accent for a Granville resident. Could have been Scottish but Tommy wasn't sure, it was deep and hoarse, he knew that much.

Who is this guy? And how does he know my dad? More to the point, how the hell does he know I don't know my dad?

Tommy's brain ticked away. He was startled. Kirsten was looking backwards and forwards between Mr Turner, Cllr Carruthers and Tommy, her mouth slightly open in disbelief.

Tommy was rooted to the spot but managed to muster some words unconvincingly, "H-How did you know my dad, Mr Carruthers?"

"Please boy, call me Jim" Cllr Carruthers said in an overly friendly manner, he turned to Kirsten and gave her a wry smile and a wink, before turning back to Tommy, "your father was a wonderful man and did great things for the young people of this town. He was a fantastic advocate for those who needed it, I miss him dearly, as I'm sure do the young people of Granville."

What the hell? Tommy was stunned. He had found out more in the last 30 seconds about his dad than he had known his entire life. He'd constantly pictured his dad as a waster, probably similar to his mum but not quite as bad he thought, but here was a respectable man telling him how great his Father was.

"I had no idea Sir, I never knew my dad; he left us when I was 2." Tommy said.

"Yes I heard he'd upped and left, no trace I believe? Such a shame. I'm sure he had his reasons; just you know that he was a man of true dedication and honour. Now, I'm not being rude, but I have to dash. Mr Turner, a pleasure as usual. Young lady, a delight to meet you," he said as he offered a slightly soft but purposeful handshake to Kirsten, "and Thomas, lovely to meet you young man, please say hello to your Mum for me."

Cllr Carruthers swiftly left Mr Turner's office. Tommy was overwhelmed by what had just happened. He had so many questions spinning around his head that he had forgotten why he was in Mr Turner's office.

"Detention for you Mr Dawson, I'm afraid." Mr Turner said with an unsympathetic smirk which brought Tommy swiftly crashing back into the room.

"But Sir-" Tommy attempted to argue.

"Would you like just one or a week's worth Mr Dawson?" Mr Turner interrupted coolly as he took his seat at his desk, put on his glasses and began working through the mound of papers in front of him.

"Just the one Sir," Tommy conceded as he motioned towards the door. His curiosity was too strong, prompting him to turn back to Mr Turner, "But Sir, who was that guy who said he knew my dad?"

"That there was Councillor Jim Carruthers, a very important supporter of this school along with many other initiatives which help the young people of this town. He has been in office for 30 years and is considered one of the nicest, most proactive professionals this town has ever seen and you'll do well to remember that you two. He's retiring this year ahead of his 60th birthday and was visiting to personally invite me to his departing ceremony." Mr Turner said with an air of pride and conviction.

Tommy thought of making a joke about Mr Turner's excitement nearly lifting the desk off the floor, but he thought better of it considering what had just happened.

Tommy and Kirsten left school and walked down Wellington Road towards Kirsten's home. The school traffic had vanished and normal service was resumed on the roads.

"How weird was that?" Tommy opened, before continuing on a bit of a ramble which Kirsten granted him the space to do so, "I mean, why did that guy mention my dad? How does he know him? I don't even know my dad! I sometimes wonder if he's out there somewhere you know, I'd love to punch him for leaving me with Tweedledum and Tweedledee mind, but part of me wonders if we'd have common interests, like music, boxing or football, you know proper Father and son stuff?"

Kirsten offered a reassuring smile and a nod for Tommy to continue if he wished. He did. He was on a roll. The cogs were turning frantically in his head, trying to piece this puzzle together.

"It's weird to think of him as a great man, my mum doesn't seem to think so, she says he left us in the lurch. I think its stranger to think of my mum with a great man to be honest. I don't even know where he went, I stopped asking her because she got upset whenever I brought it up and the 3 day binge of hysterical mood swings that followed weren't worth it." Tommy added. He could feel his eyes widen as he realised how much he'd opened up, he looked away to hide his embarrassment.

Kirsten must have sensed Tommy's vulnerability as she helped out with a subtle change of direction, "That Carruthers gives me the creeps! Did you see how he caressed my hand, ew! 'Oh pleasure to meet you my lady'" she mocked.

"I can't believe I got another detention 'coz of that prick Hargreaves!" Tommy said with an air of frustration, "I'm sick of them taking the piss because of my mum and the fact we're poor."

"Don't listen to those goons Tom, I love you just the way you are," Kirsten said.

She interlocked her arm into his as they walked, it was reassuring, although Tommy sensed it was now Kirsten who might have felt she'd overshared as she blushed rapidly and pulled her arm away again. Tommy was fiddling with his earphones and didn't respond. He heard it though and smiled inside at the show of support.

His heart fluttered a little before Kirsten quickly changed the subject yet again, "Here, pass me an earphone *Dawson* so I can listen to that with you."

CHAPTER THREE

Tommy walked Kirsten home and continued on to Brookfield's boxing gym, which was round the corner from his house in a converted warehouse on Glenwood Street. The October air was cooling now as the time pushed past 4pm and Tommy kicked his way through the dried, flame coloured leaves which littered the pavement.

He approached the boxing gym and saw the familiar site of a broken gutter hanging on for dear life, a cracked window and a shutter, which was pulled up in the summer when the weather was warm, but remained firmly down from September onwards, with a roughly sprayed warning of 'No Parking' across the middle. Despite its haggard appearance, Tommy liked it here. The door beckoned.

The familiar smell of sweaty boxing gloves and hand wraps hit him as soon as he stepped over the threshold. It was a smell that would make many people gip, but to Tommy, it was a smell that triggered feelings of excitement and security.

“Here he is, Mr Show, first name No… Where were you on Tuesday?”

Tommy smiled. The familiar voice attempting to tease him was his mentor and owner of the gym, Jack Brookfield.

“Good job I didn’t hold my breath, at my age I’d have been in trouble!” Jack continued. Tommy couldn’t help but chuckle, he could always to rely on Jack to cheer him up – and give it to him straight.

He’d been coming to Jack’s gym for a few years now. Tommy believed much of his resilience and ability to keep going was drawn from Jack and the boxing gym, which he visited on Tuesdays and Thursdays after school. He enjoyed the exercise sure, but he now realised it was also the positivity and the confidence he gained from being there that made him so fond of it.

He viewed the day that Jack knocked on his door to invite him to the gym to train – free of charge – as the day he started to develop his independence and a sense of belonging, he began to find his feet and value himself and he also started to see that there was life beyond his immediate and desolate circumstances. Tommy had known Jack from a distance as he lived only a few doors down on Frampton Road, but since training with him, he had discovered what a kind, considerate and reliable man he was, as well as being someone that you don’t mess with, despite being in his sixties.

“Sorry Jack! I was invited in to Kirsten’s house for tea straight after school on Tuesday and you know when that happens I can’t say no.” Tommy replied earnestly, as he opened his locker and removed his kit bag.

"Oh I bet you can't lad, I've seen the way you two look at each other!" Jack said, fully aware this would embarrass Tommy. Tommy blushed, his cheeks as red as the gloves he was lacing up.

"No! I meant I can't say no to her Mum's cooking – you knew what I meant! It's not like that with me and Kirsten, we're mates, best mates probably, she's cool and funny, I don't fancy her," Tommy pleaded.

"Who you trying to convince ay, young Tommy?" Jack joked, "I've been round the block a few times lad, I know what I see and I'm telling you, that girl sees you as more than a friend - and right she should might I add," a smile appearing on his face, softening his harsh northern accent. "Anyway, enough soppy talk, gloves on, in the ring, you owe me 5 rounds of pads and bar jumps for skipping Tuesday and spending it with your sweetheart."

Jack's voice disappeared off towards the other side of the room, just out of sight, where the big boxing ring was and the make-shift frame made out of lengths of old, painted scaffolding, which the gym used for bar jumps – Tommy's least favourite exercise, mainly because it was so hard and never seemed to get any easier.

Tommy looked up to argue his platonic case again, but he knew it was pointless, Jack knew how to wind him up and Tommy recognised it was all in good fun. He smiled and took himself into the toilet to splash his face with cold water, before lacing up his boxing boots.

Jack had passed the boots on to him a few months back, after one of the older lads had donated them to the gym. As with school today, he was always a little embarrassed when people gave him stuff. He didn't like to be seen as a charity case, but was grateful all the same. Tommy didn't know whether the other people at the gym knew about his home life, but Jack certainly did and was always there to offer a supportive word or two and a listening ear. He also didn't charge Tommy the usual £2 subs, always claiming that he didn't charge future World Champions or some other reason that would make him feel better about not being able to afford it.

Contrast to the crisp weather outside, in the gym the air was warm and moist and Tommy was sweating before he'd even begun his workout. The mirrors on the wall were steamed up and motivational music pumped through the speaker which was perched on a shelf outside Jack's office. The gym was old school, proper back street boxing in close, intimate surroundings. There was nowhere to hide. There were tractor tyres and beer barrels used, instead of your usual dumbbell weights, to flip, lift or throw. They had old washing line cut up into lengths for make-do skipping ropes. Gym members were expected to clean the gym, from the toilets through to mopping the floor. Tommy even had to put duct tape across a tear in one of the punch bags last week. It was a place where everybody mucked in, a real community that Tommy hadn't experienced before joining and he loved it.

Tommy enjoyed the quietness of the gym at this time, before the madness of the evening classes and the after work rush. Currently, Tommy watched on as a handful of members trained in twos or by themselves. There were two middle aged blokes sparring with head guards on in the smaller ring, looking like they were working through some defensive movement and counter punching. There was a lad hitting the heavy bag, which moulded around his gloves with every strike and was followed with a meaningful grunt. There was a man and a woman doing a circuit on the yoga mats, abs and upper body from what Tommy could tell. There was also a lady working through some technique with Jack's assistant coach, James, on the lighter bags. Tommy liked to watch the older boxers, observe and learn as Jack always taught him. At that point, Jack called Tommy over to the boxing ring and invited him in through the ropes and onto the canvas.

"Ok sunshine, we're going to work for two minutes on the pads, focussing on combinations, head movement and footwork – move that head mind, or you'll get one of these pads right round the side of it!" Jack instructed, becoming animated, "After pads, you're gonna' do one minute of hopping over the bar," Jack added, pointing over to the scaffold frame, "and then you'll get your breather. Three minutes work, one minute rest, five times... Let's go!"

They began their routine and Tommy noticed straight away that Jack was intent on keeping him on his toes to make up for his missed session, inviting some fast punching combinations and words of encouragement. He moved well for an old boy and Tommy certainly had a job keeping up with him.

Tommy would always smile when the older folk at the gym would call him Jack 'The Ghost', which apparently used to be his nickname back in his boxing days. Tommy remembers asking Jack why that was so, he'd heard it was because he was so quick that his opponents couldn't see him, but Jack would always play it down and say it was because he had a scary face.

After two rounds and several clouts round the head, Tommy could feel that he wasn't himself. He felt removed from the place that usually felt like home, his timing was off with his punches and his feet were tripping over each. He was distracted and by the look on Jack's face, he knew it.

"What's up Tom?" Jack asked during one of his minutes rest, "Look, if it's about the girl, I was only teasing you, you know that, right?"

Tommy gulped down some water and thrashed some over his head for good measure, buying time whilst he configured his response.

"Oh Jack it's nothing like that honest, I guess I'm just a bit pissed off from school today and home is a bit rubbish – but that's nothing new," Tommy said.

He felt comfortable talking to Jack about most stuff. He was probably the closest thing to a Father figure and role model that he'd had ever known. He was dying to tell him about Cllr Jim Carruthers making reference to his dad today; it was plaguing his mind still, but he couldn't find the words to bring it up, he felt a bit silly. All this time without even really thinking about it, all of sudden, he couldn't think of anything but.

"Let me guess – Craig Hargreaves?" Jack said with an air of disapproval. Jack folded his arms, resting them on his little pot belly. He had his tracksuit bottoms pulled up to his belly button so the hems were hovering off his trainers, as older people often do. His frame was slight but he carried it well, looking fit and healthy given his age. Tommy had come to realise that behind the loud and boisterous shenanigans, Jack was a sweet man with a sensitive, caring side, especially with his younger gym members.

"Yeah, he's such a wa-aste of space," Tommy said, quickly adjusting away from the actual term he wanted to use. Tommy didn't like to swear in front of Jack, he found it to be disrespectful and Jack seemed to appreciate this; one of his none negotiables in terms of conduct was to respect your elders.

"Why do you let that little jerk get under your skin? I'd love to see him come down here and take you on in the ring, pfft, if he's anything like his old man was as a kid, he'd run straight out them doors... There'd be a Craig Hargreaves shaped hole in them shutters lad!" Jack joked, he knew most the people in the neighbourhood as he'd been training kids round here for 30 years.

"I head butted him today," Tommy said, looking up with uncertainty as to how Jack would take this act of violence. Jack had always assured anybody who walked through the doors of his gym that any fighting *outside* the gym, leads to no boxing *in* the gym and Tommy had been no exception when it came to this.

Sensing Jack was trying to hide a wry smile despite him shaking his head at the news of

Hargreaves getting his comeuppance, Tommy felt safe to continue, with a slightly more down beat tone, "I got a detention as well, it was worth it though, I'm sick of him trying to bully me about my mum, or brother, or the fact I have holes in my socks!"

"Everybody has holes in their socks Tommy – otherwise how would we get our feet in?!" Jack roared with laughter and swept back his thinning grey hair. Tommy knew that this usually be would be the perfect thing to perk him up, but today, Jack's attempt to lighten the mood wasn't quite working for him and it was written all over his face.

"Look son," Jack said, with a hand resting reassuringly on his shoulder, "in life you get two kinds of people, those who *let* things happen and those who *make* things happen. Now which are you going to be? Forget those prats at school, forget your mum, although granted that's difficult as it's your mum, and rise up, use what you've got," at this point Jack poked Tommy in the temple, implying his brains, followed by his chest to signal his heart, "and make stuff happen – for you."

"Thanks Jack," Tommy said.

He smiled and put his gloves back on, ready for round three, just as the Rocky soundtrack came on. The adrenalin began to pump through his body as he stepped through the ropes. *Now we're talking,* he thought, energised after Jack's pep talk.

"Right! Let's get to work now son!" Jack ordered.

After a tough session was complete, Tommy headed to the shower in the gym, his head buzzing with praise from Jack. Whilst most would see the gym shower as an undesirable place to get cleaned up due to its infrequent visits from Mr. Sheen, Tommy saw it as a luxury – hot water *and* shower gel.

In the shower Tommy came down from the high of his exercise and plaudits and began to think about his dad again and that whirlwind fifteen minutes in school earlier. *If he was so great, why did he leave me?* He'd never really pondered it too deeply, assuming his dad wasn't worth it. But it all seemed a bit different now.

He came out of the changing rooms feeling fresh and pulled his school jumper over his head, ruffling his damp, curly hair into position.

"You'll catch a cold like that; dry your hair curly tots!" Jack said.

"What was my dad like, Jack?" Tommy said, hopeful but tentative.

"Woah, now that I wasn't expecting. Is that the real reason you've been a bit distracted son?" Jack said, rubbing his prominent chin, clearly trying to make sense of Tommy's random inquisition into his father. They'd never really spoken about it in the whole time they'd known each other and, despite the knowledge that Jack was acquainted with his dad, Timothy, and that he'd even trained him at one point, Tommy never really probed for information and likewise Jack had never really offered anything either. That was up until today of course.

"You sure you want my opinion on this, son?" Jack asked reluctantly.

"Yeah, I do. Well, I think I do. This bloke called Jim Carruthers, he's a local councillor or something, well he mentioned him today at school. He told me my dad was a great man, and did great things for kids in Granville... I had no idea and it knocked me for six, you know?" Jack gave an empathetic nod for Tommy to continue, "It's like, I'm walking along just about keeping my head above water, my dad not even on my radar and bam! Now I can't stop thinking about it. Who was he? And why the hell did he leave me if he was so great?"

"I hear you lad," Jack said, "I know Jim, he's an old friend, raised a lot of money for this gym over the years and whilst he's not said anything that's untrue, I'm not sure he should be talking to you like that about your dad, it's not his place. He probably didn't know you were so in the dark and-"

"He did," Tommy interrupted, "that's what was so weird, it's like he knew my name, who I was and knew full well that I knew nothing about my dad... It's like he brought it up on purpose, got some satisfaction out of it. I dunno', maybe I'm losing my marbles."

Tommy felt exasperated.

"I'm sure he didn't mean any harm Tom, he's a smashing bloke is Jim. He's done a lot for this town," Jack said, attempting to reassure Tommy.

"Yeah, so I've heard," Tommy muttered, before realising his tone. "Sorry, Jack. Tell me about my dad please. I've got my mum saying he's a bastard and Cllr Carruthers implying he's a legend, I'm so confused."

Jack appeared to be in thought for a second. Tommy realised that he had turned pink from holding his breath and let out a light gasp. He was on tenterhooks, anticipation making him feel a little nauseous just waiting for Jack to share information about his dad. Jack looked like he had come to terms with the situation and was ready to begin.

"Well, there's not much to say lad, other than the fact that Jim was right - he was a nice bloke, well, I thought he was but I suppose leaving your family puts that into question doesn't it? I knew him on and off for years, he was a good looking lad, got a lot of attention from the ladies in his younger days, you remind me of him at times, especially with that hair style of yours – 'curls get the girls he used to say'," Jack said, with a reminiscent smile appearing on his face. "He was a charming young man. He had his troubles, you know with your mum and everything, he tried to live life right, help others, part of me thinks that's why he fell for your mum you know, he wanted to save her. Anyway, he seemed to get wrapped up in something at work, something different. Then came long days, he became withdrawn, secretive, paranoid even. He stopped training here, distanced himself from everyone really, even your mum. She began to lose her mind – not like she wasn't half way round the block already Tom, as you can imagine – no offence," Tommy chortled. Jack was a funny man, he was straight as a dye and Tommy loved him for it.

"Then I guess something just made him up and leave - no trace, no excuse. People tried to track him down, you know for yours and Derek's sake really but that proved fruitless and they soon gave up... sorry, son."

Tommy thought for a minute as he digested Jack's words.

"I feel like I've missed out on so much Jack, this feeling is new to me. I've never given it much thought, always assumed my dad would fit the same mould as my brother and my mum, which seemed far easier to deal with than this idea that he was a nice bloke and yet still left," Tommy said, slightly disheartened. "Thanks Jack... thanks for speaking to me like an adult."

"Son, the day I disrespect you by patronising you will be the day I'm about to meet my maker." His response had conviction and reaffirmed Tommy's belief that Jack was genuine with his words. "Now you listen here, you're going to have a million and one things rushing through your mind tonight, tomorrow, probably for a good while now so remember, if you need to talk, you come here anytime and don't you forget that, ok?"

"I will do, thank you," Tommy said as he packed up his locker.

His head was spinning, a mixture of executing a perfect head butt on Craig Hargreaves, a few slaps from Jack's focus pads during training and perhaps most obviously, the unbelievable series of revelations about his estranged father had left Tommy feeling like a concrete breaker was driving its way into his skull. He made his way towards the door.

"See you later, Jack!" he called as he left the gym and hit the cold air outside, earphones firmly lodged in his ears of course.

It was getting darker now. The sun scrambled to stay up, casting light shades of auburn that smothered the rooftops of Granville. The sun's efforts were in vain as gradually it was swallowed up by the impending night time. Leafless trees swayed in the autumn wind as passers-by buttoned up their coats and burrowed their faces into their scarves to shield themselves from the breeze.

Tommy, without a hat or scarf, was unaffected by the cool night air and made his way down Glenwood Street past the abandoned warehouses, with graffiti tags sprayed onto the brick work; smiley faces. This was Smiler's area in case anybody was in any doubt. He controlled the entire town, but the graffiti was a daily reminder of who controlled each small patch and the community that lived there.

Tommy tried not to concern himself with a character like Smiler, as far as he was concerned he had nothing to do with him, despite his mum and brother probably buying drugs off him – indirectly at best, he tried to keep his nose out of that kind of business. Tommy turned onto Wood Street and eventually turned the corner onto Frampton Road towards home, although his mind seemed a million miles away.

Why did you leave Dad? He thought to himself as he paced. Despite being tired after a long day, Tommy's mind was racing and his walking mirrored this. It felt to him as though all these years, thoughts and feelings about his dad had been kept from his consciousness, contained like a reservoir behind a damn of ignorance and denial. Today that damn had burst open and he felt like he was drowning in the rush of his new found curiosity.

CHAPTER FOUR

Tommy arrived home to the sound of drunken, but joyful singing from the living room. He dropped his school bag in the small space between the front door and the bottom of the stairs. It was too small to be labelled a hall and didn't qualify as a porch. It was a space where shoes, bags and mail formed an unorganised pile, leaving little room to manoeuvre past never mind for anything else. One step to the stairs or one step to the right took you into the living room.

Tommy edged through the doorway leading to the living room, following the noise with interest. What greeted him took him by surprise and diverted his attention away from thoughts about his dad, which had occupied him on his way home. His mum and Derek were there, surprisingly upbeat and, perhaps not so surprisingly, absolutely sozzled.

"Alright you two, having fun are we?" Tommy said, his undertone of sarcasm completely missed by the pair of them.

"Tommy! Come and join us, we're having a sing song!" Theresa said, tailing off towards the end as she took a sip from her pint glass.

A cigarette clung between her fingers burning rapidly towards its demise as ash hung on, threatening to fall at any moment and add another burn to the already tattered carpet. She staggered and swayed to the sound of the Beatles' cultured tones echoing from the old CD player in the corner of the room - a contrasting juxtaposition if ever there was one.

"No, I'm ok thanks Mum, I've had a long day, just been to Jack's to train so got school work to do," Tommy said, unsure of how to feel about the sight he had come home to.

It wasn't everyday he came home to a good atmosphere - drunk yes, but singing and pleasantries, not often. He wanted so very desperately to ask them about his Dad and share with them what Cllr Carruthers had said, the catalyst to his newfound and overwhelming intrigue around his father. He read the situation and decided against it, they seemed so happy and care free, he didn't want to upset the moment and potentially start a mini riot that he could really do without.

Tommy kept his thoughts to himself, better to have the thoughts in his head at war with each other than a real life battle with his mum and Derek. He was eager to escape upstairs, put his music on and try and distract his mind from his dad. As he edged towards the door though, his mum pulled him back in and made him twirl her round. Tommy was officially part of the party. *Get me out*, he thought, as he tensed up.

There was a half empty bottle of vodka on the open brick fireplace, which had clearly been preceded by some cheap cider judging by the two empty bottles that were squished and cast aside down the side of the couch. The ashtray was piled high with singed orange butts, every last drag having been sucked from each cigarette. There was no sign of any mess associated with heroin use though, so Tommy assumed they'd caught a flight to never-never land this morning, slept it off, got up - actually managed to tidy up - and then as a reward got sloshed and began to have a boogie at some point before he arrived home.

"Do you want a drink, love?" Theresa slurred, taking a second to focus her eyes.

"No thanks Mum," Tommy said, despite the temptation. He was starting to think that a drink may well be the only way to get through this scenario – if you can't beat them, join them.

"Suit yourself." Theresa said, turning her nose up in casual contempt.

"Come on Tom, spend a bit of time with your mum and big bro, I miss you man," Derek said, revealing an alcohol infused, yet believable insight into his brother's sensitive side.

Derek shuffled over, his pencil like frame drowned by a faded and misshapen Lacoste t-shirt. He put his arm around Tommy's shoulder and rested there before leaning into his ear.

"You know I love you don't you Tom, I always have and I always will. You're gonna' make it you are, you're so much smarter than I ever was and you know your best trait? You don't give a shit about that dad of ours..."

Tommy tensed up even further. *Crikey! Of all the days to bring this up,* he thought. He lifted his head, unsure of where to focus his eyes. His mum was busy spinning herself round to Neil Diamond and wasn't tuning in to Derek's pep talk, otherwise, she most certainly would have had something negative to add about their dad.

Derek continued, his drunken voice battling with the loud music, "I applaud you Tom, 'cause me, I'm a mess, a pathetic mess who can't even get up in the morning without pills or booze, all because of him – I don't know what it is, I just can't get over it."

Despite feeling the compelling desire to correct his brother and inform him that after today, he may actually give a shit about their dad after all, this wasn't the way he wanted to discuss it. In his experience, he knew that an emotive discussion with two addicts in full flow was never going to end well, so he kept his mouth shut.

Nodding along, he struggled to find the words or enthusiasm to continue the conversation with Derek. It was dangerous territory. Yes, they were happy now, but one wrong word and the tables could soon turn towards hostility, he knew all too well.

"You know, I sometimes like to think he's a secret agent," Derek's unrelenting waffle took a bizarre but familiar turn. Tommy watched on as his brother gazed into space, presumably at the thought of his father being the next James Bond, "and I sometimes think, 'I bet that's why he had to leave', because of a secret mission you know, linked to national or international security or something!" Derek sniggered.

In situations such as this, Tommy pitied his brother. He was unsure whether Derek's delusions were drug induced from the years of consuming cocktails of substances, or was it deeper than that, that his delusions were a defence mechanism that he'd created to protect himself from the harsh truth and to cope with the abandonment.

Either way, Tommy felt guilty for wanting to leave as Derek was getting sentimental and being his very unique version of an older brother to him. It was triggered by alcohol yes, but Tommy knew Derek and knew that he meant the nice bits.

At times like this, Tommy couldn't help but remember the night he found out that his mum was a heroin addict. His memories were vivid, as though it was just yesterday. It was the day his perception of the world changed forever.

He was 12 years old, but he'd always felt that something wasn't quite right. As other Mums greeted their children home from school with a smile and a hug, Tommy was greeted with Theresa either in a drug infused frenzy or in a slump on the floor; on bad days there'd be mess to clean up too.

She had often spoken about her special medicine, he knew it wasn't Calpol, but up until this point the naive presumption existed that this so called medicine was helpful - and from the doctor. Tommy reflected fondly on his naivety and often wished he could return to that time, before he saw his world a little less rosy, before he was prematurely robbed of his innocent view of life.

He rushed downstairs from his bedroom late one night after a thud seemed to shake the house. Strange noises weren't unusual in their house; a mix of undesirable visitors, loose floorboards, drugs and alcohol often saw to that, but this particular noise set off a foghorn of anxiety within Tommy's chest. He knew straight away that something wasn't right. The same pang of worry still flared up from time to time and it took him straight back to that moment.

He could still feel his heart pounding as he remembered pacing into the living room to find his mum unconscious on the floor. He was greeted by something he hadn't seen before, but something that had become such a familiar sight in the time that had elapsed since this night. He saw the broken biro, the gas lighter and the tin foil. Back then, this wasn't as common an occurrence as it was now; his mum was still trying to keep him from her dark secret, trying to keep him from seeing her true self. *Too much special medicine*, he remembered thinking. Fortunately even as a 12 year old, he knew how to call an ambulance, it wasn't the first time he'd had to do it, but it was the first time alone.

It was the paramedics who he'd overheard talking about heroin. He'd heard people at school talk about heroin, he knew it was bad. His heart sunk whenever he thought about that moment, exactly like it did all those years ago. Apparently alcohol and Mum's special medicine, heroin, didn't mix all that well. He recalled not caring at that point about the drugs, or what it meant to have a heroin addict as a mother, all he cared about was that his mum wasn't answering to his call. He could still see her vacant face as she was whisked away into the back of an ambulance with an oxygen mask on.

Since that day, he felt that he'd become immune to the impact of his mum's drug problem. He didn't feel sorry for himself. Sure, he felt ashamed, disappointed, embarrassed, frustrated and annoyed at times. It was the elephant in the room, which had sadly become part of the family.

Truth be told, Tommy was more devastated when he realised the older brother he once looked up to so much, enjoyed the same pastimes as his mum. Despite his flaws, Derek always tried to be supportive and kind, when he was coherent of course. Unfortunately, his moments of brotherly wisdom were few and far between at best and the special moments they once shared had faded like the spark in Derek’s eyes. Tommy found it difficult to take because he loved his brother. He found that it was a little bit more of a complicated version of love between him and his mum, which is to say it wasn't really a version at all.

Derek continued to ramble on and it brought Tommy back into the room from his day dream – or nightmare rather.

“You know, I watch you Tommy and I just think, ‘he’s got some balls man!’ To get up every day, to put up with me and Mum, I know we’re a nightmare...” Derek said, appearing slightly more compos mentis than he was when Tommy first arrived home.

“Oh you do, do you?” Tommy added with a smirk.

Derek smiled, and continued, "but you do it, you keep going, to then go to school and do pretty well despite pricks like Hargreaves and his gang, as well as keeping up your boxing... well, I just think you've got it sussed, you're destined for better things than round here, floundering in self-pity with me... and her," Derek said.

They both turned to look at their Mum; the sight triggered a burst of laughter from the pair of them. They watched her in her drunken stupor, oblivious she was the focus of their attentions as her arms flayed, knees dipped and her head bobbed with her eyes closed, the stereotypical image of a dancing hippy – a drunken hippy, who was high as a kite but oddly and unusually at peace.

"Hey Derek," Tommy said, "remember when Mum used to tell us to put our pocket money into the 'special' money box under the stairs?" They both laughed.

"Yes... I was 14 before I realised it was the gas meter!" Derek snorted, before crashing onto the couch in a fit of giggles.

Tommy felt a smile spread across his face. These moments with his brother were rare. His heart sunk a little as it reminded him what he missed. *One song,* Tommy thought. *One song, I'll act like an idiot with them, for Derek's sake - and then I'm off upstairs to chill out.*

At this moment, he realised for ten minutes he'd managed to forget about his dad for the first time since Mr Turner's office this afternoon.

"Go on then Mum, turn it up," Tommy conceded, waving his mum over to where he and Derek were stood.

"Oh it's one of my favourites this, boys," Theresa said, appearing pleased that she could share this moment with her two boys, although whether she remembered it tomorrow was up for debate.

A very brief moment of peace and unity transcended upon the house for the first time in a long time. Track selection: 'Go Your Own Way' by Fleetwood Mac. Tommy, Derek and Theresa joined hands above their heads in dance and bellowed the lyrics - some correct, most mistimed, all very loud and out of tune.

Tommy laughed and sung along, Derek catching his eye. He was getting the impression that his brother was directing the words straight at him – 'you can go your own way'. The words resonated deep inside Tommy's soul; despite Derek's glazed eyes, there was a real moment of conviction and clarity in the direction of those specific words.

Classic Derek, Tommy thought, admiring his unorthodox way of being a big brother. Unorthodox or not, Tommy appreciated his brother's encouragement to strive for freedom, to spread his wings and reach his potential.

Derek wasn't always like the way he is now. Contrary to his current needy, co-dependent and reclusive state, he was once a lad about town, with lots of friends, interests and attention from the girls in the neighbourhood – Tommy always had difficulty explaining that one to anybody who didn't know Derek in his pre-heroin years.

Derek was a Wellington Road High graduate of the year 2000. He left school with a handful of qualifications, enough to allow him to enrol at college at least. He was a lively lad at school, a cheeky chap with enough redeeming features for teachers to see him as a loveable rogue rather than a little shit.

By the time he left school, Derek was heavily into smoking cannabis, drinking at the weekends and dabbling in ecstasy and the occasional bit of acid. Tommy had no clue at the time about the depth of his brother's drug use, he just saw a boy who he aspired to be like, who was popular for all the right reasons, or so he thought.

Derek's friends, Colin and Dorian, used to spend a lot of time at 10 Frampton Road and Tommy was fond of them. They'd always make the effort to chat to him and mess around. Tommy loved it. He loved gazing up at his brother and his friends and feeling that sense of pride and protection. He'd always try and cling on to whatever they were doing, which was difficult for Derek as he didn't like to let his little brother down, but it wasn't exactly appropriate to take him along so he could score. The party years continued and Derek became heavily into drugs, he'd already dropped out of college, stopped seeing Colin and eventually Dorian as much and became socially isolated. It was at this point Tommy realised his brother was hooked on heroin, not long after he'd found out about his mum.

Following this bomb shell, Tommy didn't speak to Derek for 6 whole months. He was now aware that his naivety at the time perhaps meant that he actually confused what was probably disappointment and despair with a feeling of betrayal. Over time though, Tommy had managed to ease those emotions back down towards disappointment and finally acceptance. Looking back it was clear to Tommy that Derek was a master of disguise, suppressing the inner turmoil he obviously faced around his abandonment, his lack of identity and the lack of support available to him. On the surface however, Derek used to be funny, busy and confident, although these things almost always came around through the gentle encouragement of drugs or alcohol.

Once it was out in the open and Tommy knew, his mum and Derek seemed to let standards slip. Paraphernalia would now be left casually lying around, they'd no longer feel the need to get up in the morning to give the illusion of a functioning routine in the house, strange men would come to the door as was the case yesterday evening, sometimes in the name of debt collecting for the Smiler empire, other times they'd visit to spend some time with his Mum, at which point Tommy would make himself scarce.

Derek and his mum became each other's trigger, each other's reason, each other's excuse and each other's shoulder to lean on. They didn't need to make the effort to keep up appearances anymore, so the situation at home deteriorated in free fall towards where they were at today. Tommy's view of his brother shattered into a million pieces and each time he felt as though he was putting that picture back together, piece by piece, Derek would do something that would shatter it all over again.

Despite Derek's journey down the slippery slope of drug dependency and mental and emotional frailty, he still had moments of glory like tonight; the arm round the shoulder, the pep talk and the Fleetwood Mac lyrics. These were the type of rare pieces of magic which reminded Tommy of their brotherly bond.

The song faded out and Tommy's sober cameo in the mini family party came to an end. Mum and Derek continued, changing CDs and topping up drinks. They seemed happy that Tommy had made the effort to spend some time with them, well, Derek did anyway. He could never tell with his mum.

Tommy went into the kitchen and fixed himself a slice of dry toast and a tin of mackerel with tomato sauce. There was always very few culinary options in their house, but these tins of mackerel were little gems. He would pick himself a couple up when he was responsible for the weekly shop; tasty, healthy and only 39p a go – bargain.

The mackerel on toast didn't last longer than twenty seconds as Tommy practically inhaled it. He wiped away the tomato sauce which painted his lips and brushed away the crumbs on his school shirt. Looking down he was pleased to see his white school shirt had remained intact and that he'd be able to get one more days wear out of it tomorrow.

"I'm going upstairs to do some school work," Tommy said as he passed back through the living room, fighting over the noise of Terrence Trent Darby, another favourite song of his Mum's, "have fun, you two."

"Night Tom," Derek said with a simple slur and a hiccup, "we'll try and keep it down, won't we Mum?"

His Mum didn't respond, which didn't surprise Tommy all that much. She had her ways of reminding them it was her house and she'll do whatever she pleased. Tommy smiled at Derek as he left the living room and picked up his school bag at the foot of the stairs. He took himself upstairs slowly; step by step he felt the energy in his legs drain away - Jack's boot camp earlier at the gym had certainly done its job today.

Tommy dived onto his bed, not wanting to even think about his school work, he lay back and closed his eyes. His mind slipped away as he reflected on the events of today. He thought about his mum and brother, about Kirsten and how sweet she was, about school and Hargreaves, about Jack and his training session and areas he needed to improve upon for next time, but it wasn't long before his mind drifted towards thoughts about his dad – Carruthers... Jack... *Was my dad really a nice guy? What was going on at work that changed him so much? Did Mum drive him away?* He couldn't help but feel as though something was missing.

He searched all corners of his mind for answers but all he found were more questions. It felt as though his head was in space, his eye lids were heavy and despite his eyes closing, his mind showed no signs or shutting down. His closed eyes created a landscape of blackness, beams of light shooting in every possible direction. Visions of his dad constellated all around him. He wasn't sure if the images in his mind were accurate or made up as figments of his imagination. His thoughts flew towards him, past him and all around him like a scene from Star Wars; small fighter spaceships twisting and turning, dodging in and out of one another almost colliding into a catastrophic explosion. Tommy wondered whether he'd ever get a chance to meet his dad again. Would he be the hero that Cllr Carruthers implied, or would he have his very own Darth Vader moment?

The over activity in Tommy's mind, coupled with the day's events must have tired him out as he eventually nodded off sound asleep, still wearing his school uniform - his school work still sat safely in his school bag untouched.

Tommy was usually a light sleeper, probably from spending so many nights with one eye open, worrying about who or what was carrying on downstairs below him. However, despite curiosity creating a whirlwind of uncertainty inside Tommy's head, he was able to sleep right the way through to the morning, waking only briefly, freezing cold, to slip under his frayed duvet.

CHAPTER FIVE

A week came and went in what felt like a flash. Tommy spent most of his lunchtimes at school with Mr Bishop trying to get his head around his Shakespeare assignment, which he'd managed to get handed in in the nick of time. Kirsten had helped out too after school a few nights, always round at the Cole residence as despite their closeness, he still felt conscious inviting Kirsten to his house – not because of what she would think, but because of the unpredictable nature of 10 Frampton Road and the uncertainty about what he would be bringing her home to.

One of the benefits of visiting Kirsten's house was that Tommy got to sample Mrs Cole's fabulous cooking, if he just so happened to be there at the right time, which by now he was getting pretty good at. One evening was pork and pineapple curry, a particular favourite of Kirsten's dad. He was a large man, the size of a brick outhouse, with dark skin and a big smile which lit up the room... whenever he revealed it that was. He was difficult to read, but more often than not he was nice to Tommy, although he was a little sceptical of his friendship with his daughter, as most Dads would be of their 16 year old daughters and their male 'friend'.

Mrs Cole on the other hand always made a fuss over him, she was always offering to cook him tea, make him a packed lunch, inviting him over for Sunday roast, she even asked him to stay over one night, which was rapidly over ruled by Mr Cole of course. It was clear that Mrs Cole sympathised with his situation at home and Tommy really felt a strong bond towards her. Her sympathy was never patronising or over the top, she mothered him a little but Tommy didn't mind that at all. He sometimes got the feeling that she actually wanted his and Kirsten's relationship to become a little more than friends. He'd always found this notion absurd and he usually laughed it off.

Another positive to draw from his week at school was the lack of interaction with Craig Hargreaves. Hargreaves didn't come to school the following day to the bust up and, following the weekend, returned to school a little bit more reserved than usual when in the presence of Tommy. This wasn't to say Hargreaves was an angel, far from it, he terrorised others in the playground and the classroom as usual but Tommy had noticed this week that he seemed to think twice before ruffling his feathers – whether this was a permanent fixture remained to be seen, but he was grateful for even a week of peace.

During the last week, he'd had also spent two hard sessions in with Jack on his usual days of Tuesday and Thursday. This week they spent some time on fitness and also worked on certain head movement and footwork which would allow Tommy to set up his 'brutal left hook' which Jack had aptly named. Jack wanted to enter Tommy for his first amateur boxing match at the upcoming tournament hosted right here in Granville. Tommy often wondered whether Jack's praise was genuine or a way of making him feel good – either way, it worked.

Things had been pretty standard at home this week, which is to say that his mum hadn't had a freak out that registered too far up the Richter scale. There was a wobbly moment on Monday when she had ran out of cigarettes and didn't have the money to buy more and, with it still being several hours before her benefits were paid into her account, she didn't deal with it all too well. There were a few choice words between him and his mum and even Derek got involved, although his effort at mediator was lacklustre at best and Tommy felt his brother inadvertently threw him under the proverbial bus.

His mum had tried every angle, shouting at him, pleading with him, even bargaining with him – although Tommy felt she was lacking in terms of chips to bargain with. It resulted in her storming out the house and not returning until after he'd had gone to bed – where she'd been was a mystery, although he had a few ideas. Aside from this incident, things had been on a par with most other weeks in the life of Tommy and his mum.

Other than the cigarette fallout with Mum, Tommy hadn't seen much of Derek this week, so their moment of bonding last Thursday wasn't particularly built upon. Tommy spending most evenings at Kirsten's, coupled with Derek's irregular routine, meant they'd been like ships in the night. Whenever their paths did cross, it was pleasant enough but nothing particularly out of the ordinary, which could be said to describe the week as a whole – the only difference this week being that during the times Tommy wasn't busy, or occupied, his mind had been fixated on the mystery surrounding his dad.

Today was the last Friday in October and it was a chilly one. Tommy arrived home from school to a cold and empty house. This wasn't too unusual, it either meant that his mum and Derek had had some kind of appointment to attend; doctors, dole office, chemist or drug worker – although attending their appointments with their drug workers was a more irregular occurrence than the Granville buses being on time. They always went to each other's appointments, moral support Tommy supposed, or perhaps to have a witness for how they're always 'apparently' mistreated and therefore able to defensibly whine to each other about how unfair everything was, justifying another plunge into oblivion.

If it wasn't an appointment, then it was the other thing, the thing that Tommy didn't like to think about. His mum and Derek being out together could also mean they were out scoring and if they didn't come back, it usually meant they'd gone to get their fix at a fellow addict's luxury abode, lured in by the latest batch of Smiler's products disseminated across the town. He hated the thought of his mum and Derek being completely out of it, pole axed on some random mattress in a grubby flat or house somewhere, any old random drug user passing through – he knew that desperate souls did desperate things, including his mum and Derek.

Tommy tried to forget where his mum and Derek were and what they were up to and made the most of having the use of the living room. He tidied up a little, emptied the ashtray and swept the tobacco remnants off the side, before crashing onto the sofa to watch some TV. He flicked through the channels – which didn't take long as they only had 5 – but found nothing of interest. He left Countdown on as background noise and his mind took him away back to his dad.

Tommy began wondering whether there was any way he could contact his dad. *If Mr Carruthers and Jack were right and he was such a decent guy, who perhaps left to flee the chaos surrounding Mum, maybe he'd want to be part of my life again? Maybe he lived somewhere down south, somewhere cool...Could I go and live there with him?* His mind continued to run as he day dreamed about the possibilities which would present themselves if he managed to track his dad down.

After some more day dreaming, over playing the endless possibilities in his head, Tommy made his mind up. He'd had enough of wondering, even after just one week, it was killing him – *how the hell must Derek feel after wondering for 14 years?!* He was starting to see the attraction of a life on the wrong side of normality. He had absolutely nothing to go off, but he'd decided he must try and track his dad down.

What's the worst that could happen? The confusion around his dad's credentials was driving him crazy, he felt like he just wanted to know who he was and why he left.

Tommy started looking round the house on a whim that this would be as good a place as any to look for clues. He looked in kitchen cupboards and drawers, which of course he knew were empty of any food, but he knew his mum kept scraps of paper, bills and other things in there in an unorganised and haphazard fashion.

He searched under the stairs, which was like a challenge from the Krypton Factor, sifting through brooms, the hoover, washing maidens, picture frames with no pictures, a bike helmet even though none of them had a bike and other random things which they'd felt compelled to keep but never use over the years. He wondered if his mum even knew half the stuff was there.

He drew a blank downstairs, but made the most of an empty house and scooted upstairs. He pottered around looking in his mum and brother's bedrooms, on top and inside of wardrobes, underneath beds, behind and inside the sets of drawers, he moved quickly and didn't dwell, he was reluctant to even go into his mum's room – too many jokes about looking in his mum's drawers came flooding into his head and made him cringe with discomfort. It was a no go area in normal circumstances, as he believed it should be, but this was different. The only time he ever usually went in his mum's room was to put her to bed after she'd passed out elsewhere in the house – or garden, or even street in one case.

After a quick scout around in each room, he sat on his mum's bed, head in hands and had a moment of despair. *What am I doing?*

He was losing enthusiasm already and wondered how on earth he could possibly find information for where his dad had gone, when clearly his mum hadn't had anything to go off at the time, nor did his dad's friends according to Jack – Tommy didn't even know what his dad looked like.

He felt silly and naïve for even thinking he could do this, a feeling that was strange to him. He believed he'd made large strides towards keeping his guard high, so this vulnerability was new.

Despite trying his damnedest to hold it in check, he could feel a surge of emotion making its way through his body towards his eyes, 14 years of suppressed feelings travelling at a rate of knots, dying to come out. Just as he felt he was slipping towards a desperate image of an abandoned son looking for answers, he noticed a shimmer of reflection from underneath his mum's bedside table which attracted his attention. The bedside table was worn, haggard and, like all the furniture in the house, didn't match anything else in the room, so the shine jumped out at him.

He dived to the floor at once and squeezed his hand between the small gap between the table and the floor. There was no carpet in his mum's room, it was never replaced after it got taken up some time last year due to an accident – a small fire following his mum falling asleep with a cigarette in her hand, it fell to the floor and the wiry carpet caught ablaze, fortunately nobody was hurt, the fire was contained and the carpet was the only casualty.

Reaching under the bedside table was like reaching into a hole in the wall of the Temple of Doom. Tommy brushed past cigarette butts, dead spiders, hair bobbles and those annoying hair grips which seemed to be absolutely everywhere except where they should be, his mum's hair.

After making it through the gauntlet of muck and rubbish, Tommy placed his hand on the shining object, it felt like some kind of folder with a plastic cover. He pulled it out and in his hands was an old photo album. The shimmer came from the clear plastic sheath that you could find on old fashioned photo albums. The album was a deep shade of forest green, with ornate, gold swirls on it for decoration. *Very fancy*. He'd never seen anything which looked of value or class in 10 Frampton Road. He sat up back on his mum's bed and dusted the photo album down.

He braced himself for a moment before opening it. He slowly turned the front cover to see what was inside, one eye closed with apprehension, one eye bursting open with curiosity. What he found was to his amazement. He felt fortunate that he didn't have to describe his feelings to anyone at that point as he didn't really understand them himself. He felt as though the only way to justify this moment would be for beams of golden light to burst from the book as he opened it. As he laid his eyes upon the first page, he felt a mixture of sadness, happiness and intrigue all at once. He'd found an old family photo album.

The first page contained only one photograph which was dead centre; it was his mum looking a picture of youth, a young Derek with two front teeth missing, in a baggy Le coq-sportif t-shirt, looking happy with his thumbs up. Tommy was also in the picture, as a toddler sitting comfortably and smiling in the arms of no other than Timothy Dawson, his dad.

Having never seen a picture of his dad and being too young to remember when he left, Tommy was overwhelmed. He could see that the images he'd created in his mind and dreams this last week were a mixture of subconscious memory and pure imagination. He reached out and touched the page softly, it was a distant second place to reaching out to his father in person, but it was more than he'd ever had before in his living memory.

"So this is what you look like, Dad." Tommy said to himself.

He had no time to sit and ponder however, as suddenly there was noise coming from downstairs - the front door. *Shit!* Tommy thought in a blaze of panic. He put his mum's room back to the mess it was when he found it as quickly and as quietly as he could and crept out the bedroom door. He could hear the muffled sounds of his mum and Derek downstairs as he passed across the landing on his tip toes and into his own bedroom.

Tommy pulled back the covers of his bed and buried the photo album within his bed sheets. He knew this was over precaution. In reality, he could have left it out in the middle of the floor with a giant cardboard arrow pointing at it and neither his mum or Derek would see it as they never, ever came into his bedroom; not to snoop, to clean, to even wake him for school. But today, right now, Tommy wanted to be sure that the photo album would be safe until he had time to look through it. He wasn't ready to ask his mum about it for two reasons; firstly, he didn't know what was in the album and what it meant to him right now. Secondly, how could he explain how he came across it without declaring he'd been rooting in her bedroom?

He almost fell down the steep, narrow staircase, he was that pumped with excitement. Tommy composed himself as he walked into the living room to the sight of his mum moaning to Derek about an appointment they'd just been to.

"I'm telling you now Derek, if that doctor looks at me like that one more time, I'll swing for him. Who the hell does he think he is? You heard the way he said what he said, sarcastic or what! I'd love him to spend a day in our shoes, isn't that right, son? Bleedin' self-righteous piece of sh-- Hi Thomas, you ok, love?"

Tommy's entrance interrupted his mum's rant; he was actually surprised she stopped for his benefit. Tommy noticed his mum unpacking a plastic shopping bag in the kitchen and his interest stirred a little, only to be brought crashing down by the sight of two packets of fags and a medley of boozy bottles. As usual, there was no sign of food.

"Yeah, I'm sound Mum, cheers... Just came down to let you know I'm going to be doing some school work upstairs with my earphones in, so that's where I'll be and that's what I'll be doing,"

Tommy was alarmed at how completely uncool and unnatural he was being, he was flustered by the excitement and secrecy of his discovery. His mum or

Derek didn't notice though. Derek looked up from the couch, smiled and attempted a wink as he strained to keep his eyes from rolling back. Tommy could see he was intoxicated and in one of those states where he couldn't talk, a smile was about all he could muster. He assumed his mum would be joining him soon, so being upstairs actually suited both parties - *Bonus*.

"Ok Tommy, me and Derek are just going to watch some TV and get comfortable, alright love? You ok for dinner, you can sort yourself something later can't you?" Theresa responded, eventually.

Her final question about food was typically rhetoric. He sometimes wondered what her reaction would be if he said, 'actually no Mum, can you make me something?' He'd never tried it though; he felt there was no point. He'd probably go to The Junction pub later to see Kirsten. It was her Uncle's pub and she worked there on Friday nights collecting glasses. When nobody was looking, she usually managed to sneak him a bite to eat and a few pints.

It took a while, but once his mum's secret was out in the open, Tommy soon figured out that she used the term 'getting comfortable' to refer to having a fix and conking out for a couple of hours and on this particular evening, Tommy couldn't have been happier about it. It meant time and privacy to delve into what he hoped would be the first of many clues which will lead to his dad.

"Yep, that's fine; I'll sort something out later... See you in a bit," and Tommy left, sprinting up the stairs and into his bedroom, gleefully closing the door behind him.

He dropped to his knees by his bed and burrowed under his duvet with his hands to retrieve the photo album. He whipped it out, straightened his bed, before jumping on it and sitting back onto his pillows. Tommy placed his earphones in his ears, and searched for an album on his mp3 player.

Tommy sat back and opened the photo album once more, envisioning the golden beams of light shooting from behind the front cover once more. He looked fondly again at the first page with its solo family photograph as its centre piece, before turning to look through the rest.

There were photographs of allsorts in there, pictures of them down on Granville beaches as a family, some photos of his mum and dad all dressed up on nights out, one in particular caught his eye with his mum kissing his dad on the cheek for what seemed like a laugh, he couldn't imagine his mum being so bubbly. There was a photograph of him with Derek and his dad on Granville pier carousel. It was amazing to Tommy that they had this life, compared to what he believed to be his only existence of struggle and hardship. He slowly turned page after page, the book seemed to be full of so many happy memories that he had no idea or recollection of, opening presents on Christmas day, his dad feeding him as a baby in a high chair, although most of the food seemed to be on his face and bib rather than in his mouth.

He took his time, looking at each photograph in detail. Before he knew it, an hour and a half had passed by in the blink of an eye and he was getting towards the end of the album. He was two pages from the back when he came across a newspaper cutting which looked as though it was a little out of place, like it had just been placed in there for safe keeping. Intrigued, he pulled the newspaper page out from the album and unfolded it to reveal an article which shocked him to the core. The headline read:

"LOCAL MAN, TIMOTHY DAWSON, DISAPPEARS".

He felt an immediate clang of anxiety as his chest tightened. His mouth ajar, he frantically read through the article which detailed his dad's apparent disappearance, his heart pounding like crazy. The newspaper article implied that it wasn't a simple case of husband leaving wife and kids; it implied that there was something more sinister. *Disappears...what does that mean?* Tommy thought, his head heavy with angst and confusion. *I thought he left us, why would they use that word? And if he did disappear as it suggested, why wasn't more done to find him?!*

Tommy lay back on his bed in disbelief. He lay for a second but couldn't rest comfortably enough, so sat straight back up. He re-read the article three times, slower each time. It was very cloak and dagger as newspapers often were when hard facts weren't present. It painted a picture of a loving father, married to his unstable wife, not returning home after work one evening. There was a mention of a police investigation and pleas for witnesses. It quoted his mum who said they'd had arguments leading up to it, with his dad threatening to leave. It also quoted a work colleague, who stated that he had been acting unusual at work in the weeks previous.

Tommy searched his brain for an explanation, but he came up short, he even entertained Derek's fantasy of a secret agent for a brief moment before quickly coming to his senses. Something didn't sit right. As clouds of uncertainty descended upon his mind, one thing became clear, he felt more determined than before about getting to the bottom of it, starting with his mum downstairs.

CHAPTER SIX

"Where are these questions this coming from Thomas?! And where did you even find this?" Theresa shouted defensively, groggy and cranky after being disturbed from her delightful slumber by Tommy and his interrogations.

One minute prior, Tommy had come downstairs with the newspaper article documenting his dad's 'disappearance' and asked out right for some answers. His mum was animated, up on her feet, a little dazed and dishevelled. Her pupils were like pin pricks as she attempted to come to terms with what was going on.

"Mum, no bullshit now, I want to know what happened to dad." Tommy said with forward conviction, thrusting the newspaper article in front of his mum's face as she attempted to straighten her worn dressing gown.

"Why? Why now? I've told you before, he left us! What more do you need to know? He went to work one day and never came back, leaving me to bring you and your brother up, on my own!" His mum snapped forcefully, she was backing away from his onslaught and he noticed she wouldn't even look at the newspaper.

"Look at it Mum! It says he disappeared, doesn't anything seem strange to you? Why did nobody think to look for him? Why did everybody assume he was the bad guy who left his family?! What if something terrible happened to him?!"

He fired off question after question in quick succession, as Derek stirred on the couch with a look of bewilderment. Tommy felt dazed himself; it all seemed a little surreal.

His mum retreated almost like a squirrel being backed into a corner. The only problem with a scared squirrel is - they bite!

"Do you not think I asked myself all these questions at the time Thomas?!" His mum yelled, "We had everybody round, the newspaper, the radio, the Police! Although they soon pissed off when I told them your dad had threatened to leave us on several occasions the weeks leading up to his 'disappearance'!" She was now mocking, gesturing inverted commas with her fingers. "That seemed to solve the mystery for them alright; one look at Mrs Alcoholic and the white wigs were on, judgement served!"

He could see his mum was angry now and she was firing. It was as though the scared squirrel had transformed into a bear which had been woken from its winter hibernation. The dynamic quickly changed, it was now his mum who had asserted the front foot in the argument and Tommy felt the need to begin backing away. He started to feel a little nervous; worried he'd woken the beast.

His mum's eyes were wide as she continued, "I know what they all thought, 'no wonder he left, who could put up with that crack pot!' Well you know what, I got the message loud and clear, so its time you faced it! You're dad left us – end of story, no note, no sign and no money... for 14 years!"

Derek was awake now and looking unsettled by the argument. Once he saw the newspaper in Tommy's hand, it wouldn't have taken him long to figure out what they were shouting about. Derek was giving him a look which suggested he knew exactly how he was feeling. Tommy saw Derek's head lower and his shoulders shrink as he reached for the remaining contents of his bottle of cider by the side of the couch.

"Well what about the thing at work which it mentions in the paper there? Even Jack seemed to think there was something going on at work?" Tommy asked, he was a little more subdued now.

"What thing at work?? Oh you've been asking round the neighbourhood have you? Well ask Jack bleedin' Brookfield if he can shed any light on this supposed 'work thing'? He was a pissing Youth Counsellor, what possible thing could he be involved in which would mean he had to spend every possible hour down there? If you ask me, the work thing was a front; he stayed away from here because he didn't want to be with me... Probably some young, pretty office girl down there he'd have rather been with!" His mum's words were scornful.

Blimey... Another revelation! He'd never even known what his Dad did as a job. A Youth Counsellor, he was surprised and impressed, although he had no time to revel in his Dad's choice of career at this moment in time. Tommy could see his mum genuinely believed his Dad left them all those years ago and it had torn her apart ever since. He wondered if she'd always been so sure, or did she start out feeling like he was now; uncertain, sceptical, optimistic almost. Perhaps she had just retold the story in her head – and heart – that many times over the years that she was eventually convinced it was as straightforward as him leaving them. Let's face it, Dads up and down the country, all over the world even, walk out on their families without a trace. *Could my mum be right?*

"So why did the newspaper say he disappeared?" Tommy asked. He felt he was pushing his luck a bit with his questions. His mum was losing her patience, possibly itching for a drink and certainly desperate to end this conversation. He was fortunate in a sense that it wasn't a few more hours later and she'd have had the heroin withdrawal to contend with too.

"Tommy, newspapers will say whatever they can just to sell copies, don't be so naïve, Son." She said, surprisingly a little calmer than her previous response. She seemed to be over her anger and defensiveness and transitioning towards being upset and exhausted with it. She sat on the couch next to Derek, who looked about as uncomfortable as anybody could, and put her head in her hands.

Tommy continued, "I'm just so confused Mum, don't I deserve to know? You make out he was this bastard, but yet I've just found out he was a youth counsellor, Jack said he was a nice guy when I asked about him and Councillor Carruthers said he was a great man?"

Before he could carry on, his mum's head darted up instantly and looked Tommy straight in the eyes. At that moment, he knew he'd pushed it too far. She jumped to her feet from the couch, radiating a wired kind of energy.

"Who said he was a great man?" she said with venom and sharpness in her words, glaring as she spoke.

"Councillor Jim Carruthers, a bloke who I met at school last week, he's been on the local coun—"

"I know exactly who he is Thomas, his face is on the posters that are up in every fucking place in this town, radio adverts, the news, he's everywhere shouting about how he's done this and that for the town – fat lot of good it's done us... Now, let me ask you this... Why were you talking to him and what the hell has your dad got to do with it!?"

His mum had turned blank behind the eyes. She wasn't hysterical like she normally goes when she's upset, she was calculated and borderline deranged. Tommy was unnerved by the coldness his mum was displaying.

Nervously, Tommy responded, "I was in Mr Turner's office and he was there, something to do with his 60th birthday and retirement. Anyway he mentioned my dad and him leaving, said he was a great man and he missed him... He also said say hello to your mum for me, which was weird."

"GET OUT!" His mum erupted uncontrollably, "Coming in here with your newspaper articles and your hot shot councillors thinking you know all about your dad now, do you? Well, why don't you piss off out of here and see if they'll help you get some answers, because clearly Thomas, me and Derek here aren't good enough!"

Tommy was stunned. He knew it was futile to even try to argue or even discuss the matter further and frankly, he felt too shocked and worried to do so anyway. His mum had gone, fuse blown, plot lost. She stormed into the kitchen and poured herself a large vodka, a measurement reaching over half way of her favourite tumbler glass with no mixture. She picked up the glass that had a faded picture of Bart Simpson on the side, her hand shook as she tipped the contents straight down her throat – Tommy didn't even see her swallow. She lit a cigarette, her staple response to any situation, staring ferociously back at Tommy the whole time.

Tommy was a little bemused at the escalation, he looked to try and gain some kind of support from Derek but, as usual when it came to arguments with his mum, he stayed neutral, offering only a sympathetic shrug of his weedy little shoulders. Tommy headed for the door, not even stopping to grab his coat.

It was 8:30pm now as Tommy made his way through the cold October night towards the Junction pub. Kirsten started her shift at 7pm and usually finished around midnight. Tommy often went to see her on a Friday night, she could squeeze in a few breaks throughout the night and her Uncle was pretty cool about him being in there, despite being under age.

Tommy walked at a quick pace, his breathing heavy as he recovered from the blazing argument which had just occurred. *What just happened?* Adrenalin rushed causing his body involuntarily spasm as he processed his thoughts. His brain was fried as he tried to reflect on what he knew so far. He couldn't make sense of it all.

On one hand he had his mum's view that his dad had upped and left after threatening it for a few weeks, fed up of her and her ways. On the other he had this new idea of him being a great man created by Cllr Carruthers and Jack, coupled with the fact he had now learnt his dad was a youth counsellor. Two things niggled at him about the whole situation. Firstly, his mum's explosive reaction just now which he found to be strange, and secondly, the newspaper article – TIMOTHY DAWSON DISAPPEARS. It just didn't add up. He couldn't wait to offload to Kirsten.

Tommy's house was on the edge of the Fulton estate, by the main road. The Junction pub was right in the middle of the estate, so his journey consisted of meandering through the small streets, alleys and across overgrown, grassy areas.

He passed a handful of dodgy looking characters, drunks and hoods, low level drug runners for Smiler probably; you could tell they weren't in the higher ranks because everybody knew that with progression through the empire came a tattoo of a smiley face on the neck behind the ear - a stamp of ownership disguised as loyalty, etched into the skin for eternity. Plus, only low level runners would be out on the street on a Friday night. They stared as Tommy nervously walked by, no tattoo, so plenty to prove – *dangerous*, Tommy thought. He felt tense and noticed he'd closed his fists and clenched his teeth as he approached.

Despite the eagle eyes of Smiler's troops, Tommy's walk was relatively uneventful. It was mainly quiet on the estate tonight, although it was still early and way before kicking out time at the Junction. Tommy cut through the ginnel which led up to Hale Avenue, the Junction pub was on the corner, glowing and vibrant in the dark night, a hideaway of activity which was a home away from home to many of the folk on the estate.

The hustle and bustle of a Friday night in the Junction greeted Tommy as he walked in and made his way to the far end of the bar where Kirsten's glass collection station was. The noise level in the pub was that loud, he could barely focus his ears on any one thing in particular, but it was a noise that was comforting.

He perched himself on a bar stool and waited, she hadn't noticed him yet. He watched on as she busily loaded the small glasswasher with her back to him, her hair was tied up in its hive of curls, she had her black pants on which hugged her figure and a black polo shirt on with 'The Junction' in white letters across the back.

Tommy found himself smiling as he watched his friend work away, oblivious to him watching on. He thought she looked cute and was almost bordering on checking her out, before he quickly stopped himself – *What are you doing?* He thought, as he dragged his eyes away from Kirsten, questioning whether he may actually be attracted to his best friend - *Not a good time Tommy!* He reminded himself.

Kirsten shut the glasswasher door and turned to face the rest of the pub, her eyes drawn straight to Tommy.

"Hey you!" she said, waving as she spoke, "I'll be over in five, just got to clear a few more tables." Kirsten smiled that beautiful smile. She always looked so happy to see Tommy and tonight, he needed that more than ever.

Tommy turned on his stool to have a look around the pub. Kirsten's Uncle Bill gave him a nod from the other end of the bar as he pulled down on a real ale pump. Joan Markey and her toy boy lover were smooching in one of the window seats. There were a few of the lads who had been a couple of years above him at school over by the pool table, joyfully shouting and laughing with each other. The atmosphere was good in the pub; he'd almost forgotten what had happened at home.

"Alright there, young Tommy!" came a familiar voice from behind him and a hand on the shoulder. He turned to see one of his brother's oldest friends, Dorian.

"Dorian! How you doing, mate?" Tommy said enthusiastically.

He always liked bumping into Dorian; he had fond memories of growing up with him around.

Dorian pulled up a bar stool next to him for a chat. This was one of the things he liked about him, he felt as though he didn't just see him as Derek's kid brother; he actually seemed to see him as his own person, with his own story and his own attributes.

"I'm good cheers, all the better for seeing you man, how's things?" Dorian asked with seemingly genuine interest, "Do you want a pint?" he said and before Tommy could answer, signalling the bar lady for two pints of Carling.

"Things are good thanks Dorian, well you know, as good as can be," he said, airing on the side of caution after the bust up at home he'd just walked away from. Not cautious enough however.

"Let me guess, your mum?" Dorian said with a smile. Dorian was one of those people who called your bluff and he'd called Tommy's in an instant. He knew the situation at home and could see that despite Tommy's valiant efforts, something was bothering him.

Dorian was slightly below average height, it seemed strange to sit next to him now having been so used to looking up at him all these years, Tommy now had to look down slightly. Dorian's hair hadn't changed much, it was dark brown, the fringe sweeping across his forehead. He had ears which stuck out a little, and freckles on his nose. He was smartly dressed as Tommy always remembered.

"Yeah, to be honest I've just had a blazing argument with her at home, made the error of asking about my dad..." he said, mindful that he was showing a little vulnerability. Dorian looked down and shook his head a little before responding.

"Tom, listen, promise me you won't go down that road? I watched your brother drive himself to the brink of despair over your dad; Derek's still not found his way back to normality, has he?" Dorian said, with Tommy shaking his head. "It's not worth it, mate. Trust me. Concentrate on what you've got, focus on school and get out of this dump we call a home!" Dorian added, with an infectious laugh.

The bar lady who served Dorian was new and as she planted two pints on the bar, she gave a suspicious look at Tommy. She looked over at Bill for guidance, who signalled that it was fine for Tommy to drink in here and Dorian paid her. Tommy breathed a little sigh of relief and took a keen sip of his pint.

"Feels weird sharing a drink with you in the pub, Tommy, I can remember you as a kid, taking you for your first kick about, babysitting for you, seems like yesterday that stuff," Dorian said.

Tommy laughed, "I know it's weird, isn't it," he said, "I can remember those times, always seemed so fun."

"So, go on, I better ask... How is he, that donut of a brother of yours?" Dorian asked, knowing full well what the answer would be.

"The same really, not much has probably changed since you last saw him. He and my mum still live day to day, drinking, getting high whenever they can. Now I'm old enough to look after myself, I just leave them to it. We've managed to find some kind of normality, which usually keeps the peace – well, until today."

"Mate, the day that's normality is the day you need to get the hell out!" Dorian joked.

Tommy didn't mind Dorian making light of it; in fact, he appreciated it as it made it less awkward. Plus, he knew the situation as well as anyone.

"I've not seen him for over a year you know? I'm in the Royal Air Force now. It's the best thing I've ever done Tom, I swear to you. Pay is good, I get to see the world and I don't have to deal with the bullshit that comes with living in Granville."

Tommy swooned at the thought of moving away and seeing the world. *No more Granville...* They continued to chat and joke, reminiscing about the old days and Dorian telling new tales of his adventures with the R.A.F, before Kirsten came over to join them.

Dorian smiled, introduced himself briefly, before politely excusing himself to re-join – and rescue – his friend, who he'd left round the other side of the pub in the hands of 'Crunchy', a regular called Roy Carrot. Crunchy had a reputation for being able to talk a glass eye to sleep, so Dorian's friend was probably cursing him for leaving him so long.

Dorian gestured to Tommy about Kirsten as he left giving him the thumbs up, but Tommy shyly shook his head.

"You look happy," Kirsten said with a smile as she took a seat on the stool that Dorian had just vacated.

"Yeah, I wasn't before I came in here though," he said. Tommy noticed Kirsten smiling and blushing slightly; he suddenly became flustered and for some reason felt compelled to keep just talking in an attempt to play down what Kirsten had clearly read from his initial comment. "You know, catching up with my brother's old mate… and seeing you of course."

Damn it! Tommy looked down at the bar; his attempt at avoiding an awkward situation in actual fact became the contributing factor in creating one.

"So, what have you been up to?" Kirsten said, moving the conversation on.

"Arguing with my mum, it was awful Kirst, honestly, she freaked out…"

Tommy told Kirsten all about the evening's events. Starting from the photo album, to the discovery of the newspaper article and that headline which bugged him so much, to him breaching the subject with his mum and her flying off the handle at the mention of Jack Brookfield and Councillor Carruthers referring to his dad as a decent guy. Not forgetting the fact his dad is a Youth Counsellor by profession, which Kirsten agreed was pretty cool.

Kirsten listened attentively as she usually did and it was just what he needed. She gasped on cue and offered him supporting words when needed. When he'd finished, she nipped behind the bar to get him another pint of Carling. She thought she was being so stealthy, but Tommy could see it was so obvious that her Uncle Bill knew exactly what was going on.

Just like her Mum, Tommy felt as though Kirsten's Uncle Bill liked him. He knew his story and had a soft spot for him; again, it wasn't patronising sympathy, it felt more like a kind of respect, presumably for getting on with his life despite his circumstances. Bill also seemed to share Mrs Cole's view that there could be more than friendship between him and Kirsten as he made wind-up jokes on the regular to tease them.

"You drink that, eat those and watch the end of the football on the TV, whilst I just whip round and clear the glasses. I've got to sort the kitchen out as well, then I'll get a proper break at 10pm, we'll chat more then." Kirsten said as she returned.

She placed down the frosted pint glass that was filled with fizzy lager, the bubbles racing towards the top only to be suffocated by the thick frothy head. She also threw him a bag of salted peanuts and some Quavers, before rushing off to get back to work. Tommy was grateful for the snacks as he was so hungry his stomach hurt – the drinks were a nice bonus too. He wolfed down the bar snacks and took a few sips of his ice cold pint of lager. He felt so grown up and it felt nice.

10pm came around soon enough and Kirsten was back with her own drink in hand – a Bacardi and diet coke, which she passed off as being *just* diet coke. She'd had a couple during her shift so was a little tipsy, as was Tommy as he slurped back half of his third pint. They made their way over to a table, which was out the way, just by the jukebox. They chatted some more, mainly about Tommy's intrigue into his dad, before eventually moving on to other topics; school, aspirations, life.

A few drinks later and the pair of them were fully relaxed now and talking openly. Tommy was so comfortable in Kirsten's presence and it seemed as though the feeling was mutual. Tommy noticed that Kirsten was fixing her gaze on him a little longer than she normally did and he liked it. *God, she's beautiful*, he thought, *why have I never noticed it before?*

Kirsten got up and put some coins in the jukebox. Track selection: 'Up the Junction' by Squeeze. This track always went down well in the pub, for obvious reasons. Squeeze were one of Tommy's favourite bands and Kirsten knew it. They were an old band from the 70's and 80's that he'd discovered after finding an old tape cassette in his house some time ago. He instantly warmed to them, he'd played their songs to Kirsten a few times and he liked to think she was warming to them too – maybe tonight's song choice proved that to be the case – or maybe Kirsten was being typical Kirsten and doing everything she could to cheer him up.

As the intro reached its iconic drum rudiment, Tommy laughed and gave Kirsten a playful clap for her choice of song. To Tommy's surprise, she pulled him up out of his chair and tried to get him to dance. Embarrassed but tipsy enough not to care, he allowed it to happen and went with the flow. They had a little bop around by the jukebox, much to the amusement of the rest of the pub goers.

The song finished and last orders were called. Tommy sat down, his head in a pleasant spin. Kirsten swept up their glasses from the table as she headed back to work to do her final round of glass collecting. Tommy watched her as she walked away, he couldn't help it but his eyes were fixed on her in a way they hadn't ever been before. Before he could get a hold of the situation, he was alarmed to see her turn around and catch him in the inexcusable act of checking out his best friend. He offered an awkward smile, but he was sure he'd been busted. His fears were immediately alleviated however when she giggled and smiled right back.

Eventually the pub cleared of the Friday night crowd. Kirsten's Uncle Bill let Kirsten go a little earlier and as she was putting on her jacket, Tommy approached Bill a little timidly at the bar as he was cleaning the lines.

"Thanks for the drinks tonight, Bill," he said, with genuine appreciation.

"Don't you worry lad. I'll stick it on your tab, yeah?" Bill joked, as they walked towards the door. Tommy and Kirsten laughed as they exited, he was pretty sure Bill was kidding seeing as he didn't have a tab nor could he afford one, but he never could quite tell.

As the bitterly cold October air hit them, Tommy quickly realised that leaving the house in a hurry earlier had come back to bite him. He'd not picked up his jacket and wore only a thin jumper and truthfully, it had seen better days. He waited as Kirsten took a cigarette from her bag and lit it – a habit she'd developed after having one or two drinks.

"Thanks for listening to me tonight Kirst," Tommy said, "Feel like all I've done is go on about my dad this last week… I just want to know what happened to him, you know? That newspaper article about him disappearing has shaken me up, it's all a bit fishy to me and I'm determined to find out what happened."

Before Kirsten could displace the cigarette from her lips to respond, a faceless voice came from the shadows.

“Be careful what you wish for, boy.” said the voice. It was creepy and made the pair of them freeze, rooted to the spot.

A figure appeared from the pitch black alley which ran down the side of the pub. The voice belonged to a man who appeared old and haggard but he stood in a position which meant that only half of his face and body could be seen from the limited light available. He seemed like a shifty character, a man who was on edge. He kept looking around over his angular shoulders, like he was scared to be seen. His face was shaded so it was difficult to even tell what he looked like really, other than the fact he had a beard and he didn’t look like he took much care of himself.

“Excuse me, do I know you?” Tommy said, a mixture of Dutch courage and nervousness making him uncertain of what to make of the old man.

“I very much doubt it boy, but I know you... and I knew your dad, Timothy too. I heard you grumbling in there and just now out here about the mystery surrounding your dad. It’s quite a situation you’ve got yourself there young Thomas. I’m here to give you a shilling’s worth of free advice, I’ll say it only once... Don’t go asking questions which have answers you won’t want to find.”

The man’s words were cold and prickly, sending chills down Tommy’s spine enough to make each vertebrae shudder. The situation made even more intense by the fact he stood in the shadows and made no attempt to reveal himself.

“What do you mean? Do you know what happened to my dad?!” Tommy enquired swiftly, edging closer to the man. He had found a little more challenge in his voice now, leaving Kirsten a few steps behind him, uneasy and quiet.

"Not exactly, I knew him at the time though. Let's just say not everything is always as it seems. Right now, I'm guessing you're starting to think your dad was this great guy and that maybe he didn't leave you and your brother, huh? Well, if you do decide to start snooping around in the past boy, you better be prepared for some surprises. If you put your hand into a pit of snakes, you're bound to get bitten, know what I mean?" The old man's cryptic tale was worrying Tommy and created yet more questions.

"So why tell me this? Why talk in riddles, if you know something, tell me!" Tommy demanded, impatiently, taking another couple of strides forward.

"Don't get too close! I'm only here to give you a friendly warning, boy. I'm not here to get involved; I made that mistake a lifetime ago. Even just knowing your dad back in the day led to me losing my job, which meant I lost my house then my wife. I've never seen him since to thank him!" The man said with an ironic chuckle, "Your dad was involved in something which pissed off the wrong people! You start asking questions, it won't be long before word gets round, understand?"

Tommy listened intently to the old man and hung on to every word and, now that he had managed to get a little closer, he realised he perhaps wasn't as old as he first thought, probably late forties. Tommy turned to Kirsten,

"See what I mean Kirst, something's not right..." But as Tommy turned back to respond to the old man, he had disappeared back into the shadows. Tommy darted over towards the alley where the old man came from, but it was dark and he couldn't see anything.

"Where did he go?" Tommy said desperately confused, "Did you not see him go?!" he asked Kirsten in disappointment, before shouting down the alley, "Hello! Hey old man! Come back, you can't just leave, I need answers!"

His voice echoed as he peered into the darkness. He strained his eyes, desperately trying to seek out the old man. He could feel the damp moss under his feet as he edged closer into the alley.

Kirsten moved over to him and put her arm round him gently; her touch made him jump a little. He was shivering, probably freezing cold, but the adrenalin felt as though it was masking it for now. It wouldn't last though and he knew that to stay out without a coat in this temperature, weather chasing a shadow, wouldn't be wise.

"That was so weird," Kirsten said, attempting to guide him away from the alley. "Come on Tom, let's get out of here, that guy gave me the creeps! Walk me home please, we can talk about it on the way, let's just get moving."

Her words comforted him a little, but he felt shell-shocked. His head buzzed with surreal confusion. They slowly walked off in the direction of Kirsten's house, linking arms and propping each other up slightly.

Tommy checked over his shoulder several times in disbelief, before eventually the pub was out of sight and the only way place he could now find the strange man from the shadows, was by playing it over and over in his mind.

CHAPTER SEVEN

Tommy didn't get much sleep that night. He tossed and turned and drifted in and out of consciousness, back and forth between frustrating thoughts and mind bending dreams. He even had to change his bed t-shirt in the night due to the cold sweat which poured out of him. His heart and head rushed from one thought to the next, racing with no rhyme or reason.

His mind was saturated with random images of his dad, his mum, the faceless man in the shadows outside the pub earlier that night, drug dealers who visited his house, Jack, Cllr Jim Carruthers, his school teachers, Kirsten, Hargreaves, Derek all swirled into a distorted nightmare trying to piece together this mysterious story, always returning back to the same question – *What on earth happened to my dad?*

Despite it being a Saturday and his eyes dark and heavy, Tommy couldn't wait to get up and out of bed once morning arrived. The frustrating night's sleep had left him twitchy and anxious. The man in the shadows at the pub the previous evening had created a new dimension to the story around his dad's disappearance and Tommy could come to no other conclusion than something bad had happened. The way he saw it, too many things didn't add up and, despite the warnings heeded the previous evening, he felt duty-bound to keep digging.

It was only 8am but Tommy had been up and pacing his bedroom for a good hour. He was making notes and scribbling things down in the back of a school note pad. He was trying to build a picture of the story behind his dad's disappearance; names, places, time lines and key points which had surfaced this last week.

So far there were three distinct areas; his mum and the turbulent relationship with arguments prior to his disappearance, work and the superlatives received by Jim Carruthers, building a picture of him as a conscientious man, plus this mysterious 'thing' which had presented itself in several ways – the newspaper article, the man outside the pub and Jack Brookfield's view that he became involved in something which consumed him prior to his disappearance. There was still so much he didn't know, he needed to find out more pieces to the jigsaw.

Tommy knew he'd find no answers in his bedroom, so he got dressed and decided to head out. Jack's gym opened at 9am on a Saturday, he fancied blowing off some steam and attempting to get a hold on this nervous energy, so he thought about starting his Saturday down there. Plus, he could always try and lean on Jack for more information.

Tommy left his bedroom and went out onto the landing. Other than the odd creak of a floorboard, the house was still and deathly silent; he presumed Mum and Derek would be conked out in bed as he'd heard them stumble around the house at around 4am, their attempts at being quiet non-existent, as they helped each other crawl up the stairs and into bed.

When Tommy returned from the Junction last night, they were just getting ready to 'cook-up' as they called it. His interruption stalled and unsurprisingly flustered them as they made a hash of covering up their deed, but he knew the signs and could see what was going on even in a split second. Not wanting to disrupt them and desperate to avoid another head on collision with his mum, they exchanged a quick and emotionless glance before he swiftly bypassed the living room and went straight up to bed, leaving them to crack on with their rituals – which clearly by this morning's lack of activity in the house went exactly to plan.

He tentatively peered around Derek's bedroom door and was greeted with pitch black darkness and the rotting smell of a 23 year-old heroin addict. There was no sign of movement, although by the look of Derek's crispy socks, which were almost self-standing in the middle of the floor, there was every chance that they could walk themselves to the washing machine any minute. He repeated the same routine in his mum's room and found the same outcome, with a slightly less intense smell. He was just about to head down the stairs when something caught his eye – the hatch to the loft.

He hesitated as his intrigue took over. His desperation for clues had him suddenly wondering, hoping and believing that the loft could be his very own Pandora's Box.

Tommy backed up onto the landing and stared up at the loft hatch, a place he didn't think to look the other day on his frantic search around the house, which culminated in the discovery of the photo album and the bizarre newspaper article. He'd never been up to the loft, never needed to, it barely registered with him that they even had one. He had no idea what was up there, he assumed whatever it was, was old, dusty and buried in the past – the perfect criteria for another clue on his quest. His curiosity was lit as he imagined the possibilities.

After quietly manoeuvring the chest of drawers from his bedroom and positioning it directly under the loft hatch as a make shift platform, Tommy stepped up and lifted the hatch door out of place and slid it across into the abyss of the loft, allowing his head to pop up and get a sneak peek at what was up there. Nothing. Or at least that's what his eyes could see as it was pitch black.

I need a torch! Tommy steadily climbed back down from his perch and made his way softly down the stairs. He returned moments later after remembering he'd stumbled upon an old torch amongst the clutter under the stairs that he'd sifted through yesterday.

Tommy climbed back up onto the chest of drawers, careful to remain as quiet as he could, and flashed the torch up into the loft. What greeted him didn't live up to his hopeful expectation. Granted he didn't quite expect to see a police evidence board up there with the story mapped out, documenting clues, timelines and suspects, but he'd expected a little more than what he saw. He slowly scanned the room, beady eyed with torch in hand as he craned his neck through the hatch door. He saw joists, furry insulation barely still attached to the roof and the big copper water tank. He was close to giving up when something in the far left corner caught his eye. It looked like a cardboard box, inconspicuous at best, but Tommy thought it was worth checking out.

Placing the torch in between his teeth, Tommy hoisted himself up into the loft – those bar jumps and circuit training sessions at Jack's gym had paid off as it caused him little trouble at all. He positioned himself onto one of the joists and dusted himself down. He had to stoop over due to the low roof as he began to traverse across to the other side of the loft.

His balance wasn't the best; he knew that one wrong move could lead to a foot going straight through his mum's bedroom ceiling and a hell of a lot of explaining to do. His legs shook with a mixture of excitement, adrenalin and blind panic. Beads of sweat began to form on his back and forehead as he drew closer to the cardboard box.

He was a matter of inches away when his foot suddenly slipped off the wooden beam. He panicked as the image of him crashing through the plasterboard below and onto his mum's bed in the room beneath flashed before his eyes. He reached out for anything, which fortunately for him was a joist above that was part of the roof and kept him just about upright.

He survived the fall and regained his composure, but in doing so, he dropped the torch. A dull thud echoed around the empty loft room as the torch hit the plasterboard. It rolled away as Tommy looked on in despair. He waited, listened for any sign of life below... Nothing moved. Mum and Derek had not been woken from their slumber and relief flooded his body. Tommy repositioned himself securely onto one joist, squatted down and recovered the torch before shining it down on the cardboard box.

He blew hard across the surface of the box contents and revealed a mixture of items; old trophies, a couple of books, some cassette tapes, an old Panini sticker album from 1981, a piece of pottery with the initials 'TD' engraved but yet Tommy had no recollection of ever making such an item, before finally he pulled out a picture frame and wiped away the dust and muck which smothered it, revealing a certificate for a counselling qualification – it was a box of his dad's old stuff.

Tommy couldn't hide the smile on his face once he'd realised what he'd discovered. He wasted no time in packing the box up and cautiously made his way back across the beams, box in hand, carefully lowering himself through the loft hatch and back into the safety of his own bedroom so he could explore further.

The box was clearly old as it was tatty and damp and the stuff inside wasn't in much better condition. After closing his bedroom door behind him, Tommy perused through the items, smiling as each one revealed a little bit more about his dad. There were old photos in there, an old football scarf, a medal from boxing - Tommy couldn't believe how they had such similar interests. His heart gushed as he finally found a sense of belonging, whilst simultaneously breaking as it was found in a tatty, old cardboard box and not personally from the man he wished he could have known. All of these years he'd been blissfully ignorant of who his dad was and what could have been. He felt emotional, as a sense of unfairness overwhelmed him, a feeling during his life that he'd worked tirelessly not to succumb to.

Poking around with the last few items, Tommy came across a black, leather bound note pad. As per the other items in the box, he blew the dust and cobwebs away and opened it up with interest. What he saw almost sent him jumping back up into the loft that he had just come down from. His heart beat uncontrollably as his eyes frantically absorbed the information as quickly as was humanly possible. The black leather bound book was a note pad containing notes from what appeared to be his dad's work life.

As Tommy read through the black leather bound note pad his eyes widened in disbelief. The book contained detailed, secret notes documenting cases of which his dad had been involved in at work. He brushed his hand across each page as though to check it was real and read the contents as fast as his eyes could keep up.

Upon second reading, Tommy was starting to think that there were a couple of strange things about these notes. Most notably perhaps, was that the notes didn't seem to be that professional, considering they were work related notes. They looked more like scribblings, almost as though they were his dad's own personal notes, possibly the kind a private detective would do. *But why was he writing these notes? What was my dad doing?*

Tommy began to piece bits of information together and make sense of the notes. He figured out that each page told the brief story of a young person that had clearly come to his dad for counselling all those years ago. There were the stories of Julia Stark, Brendan Gould, Jennifer Jefferson, Kenny Morrell and Katie Beardall.

As Tommy read through it became clear why his dad had picked these particular five to investigate – *or whatever he was doing*. They all had one thing in common. Besides having his dad as their counsellor – they had become involved in Granville's infamous drug scene at the age of 14… and they had all died before their 16th birthday. There were graphic details given for all of their deaths including suicide and murder. The only one who differed slightly was Katie Beardall's story. Tommy noticed that information surrounding her fate was brief, stating merely that she was 'presumed dead'.

All of a sudden it hit Tommy like a sledge hammer… These notes weren't standard, run of the mill case notes; they were notes which documented his dad's suspicions around these unfortunate deaths. Tommy was frozen solid in utter astonishment; he had no idea what he should do or how he should feel about this huge discovery, but the man from the outside of the pub's drunken ramblings the previous evening were now starting to seem a bit more coherent than he'd initially hoped. *This must be the thing that consumed him!*

Tommy read through the notes once again, case by case. He thought reading them again would ease his tensions and anxieties but it only heightened them further. He saw how and more importantly *why* his dad had been suspicious – there were scribbles and arrows, notations and things heavily underlined indicating his dad's thoughts; their age, their habits, the fact that both Julia and Kenny had been found hanged, neither having mentioned suicidal thoughts to his dad in their previous counselling sessions. Brendan was found stabbed on Lostock Park, another estate within Granville, with no killer ever found or brought to justice. Jennifer was found having overdosed on what was apparently a strong batch of heroin, despite his dad's belief that she didn't even take heroin, just party drugs such as ecstasy and amphetamine. There was still a question mark hanging over Katie's fortune however, with no notes around her death, just a big question mark after the words 'WHERE IS SHE? CAN I SAVE HER?' *What the hell happened to these kids?*

Tommy's determination for the truth felt stronger than ever before. He turned the final page of notes to reveal a page had been ripped out. Tommy thought for a second and, not wanting to be defeated by a pesky torn out page, he had an idea. Noticing that there was indentation on the blank page below, Tommy used some detective skills he'd picked up watching Colombo on Channel 5. He scrambled around for a pencil and used it to shade across the paper, revealing the text that had been written on the ripped out page.

ONE PERSON IN COMMON - SMILER!

A sudden panic hit Tommy – *Smiler!* Just when he thought the situation couldn't get any worse, a stick of dynamite was thrown into the mix with the word 'Smiler' written right down the side of it. *What did you do with this information, dad?* He wanted to stay positive but he connected the dots and feared the worst kind of outcome, considering his dad disappeared not long after the dates in this notepad.

Tommy reluctantly began to wonder if his dad had suffered the same fate as the young people he'd been trying to save, it seemed to make so much sense. He raised questions about the suspicious deaths of kids and then is gone without a trace. This was surely too much to be a coincidence.

A ton of bricks came crashing down all over Tommy. His thoughts were erratic and full of dread. He raced to conclusions, starting to believe that his dad must have discovered all those years ago that the most notorious villain in Granville had been involved in the deaths of the young people he'd been working with through counselling. More devastatingly however, if this was the case and his dad went public with this information, Tommy himself could have just discovered that the very same villain had been responsible for the disappearance - or worse the death - of his own dad.

Tommy was well aware that the urban legend surrounding Smiler was very much alive and active; he assumed a person in his power couldn't be so for so long without having certain law enforcement personalities in his back pocket, he'd heard the stories, he knew how it worked. He wondered now whether his dad felt the full consequence of crossing the sick and twisted power of Smiler.

Tommy was at a major crossroads in his quest to find out what happened to his dad. Did he continue along this road with the risk of rustling the wrong feathers, much the same as his dad had appeared to do? Or did he ignore the signs and go back to the safe but painful ignorance of never knowing what really happened to his father?

Ignore it? How can I?

Perseverance and bravery was stirring inside of him. He needed to talk to somebody and there were only two people he trusted with this information. He knew Kirsten was out shopping with her Mum this morning, so he headed to his boxing mentor and friend, Jack Brookfield, to seek a calming influence and try and make sense of this potentially devastating and life changing information. One question fought its way to the front of his mind above all the others – *Who the hell is Smiler?*

Tommy threw the black note book into his school ruck sack, along with his boxing kit – although he didn't think he could concentrate long enough to lace his gloves never mind do any training – and headed down the stairs and straight out the door, pacing like a man on a mission.

It was a fresh morning outside, with the low autumn sun peeking behind the brick chimneys on the rooftops. Tommy stepped onto Frampton Road and headed in the direction of Jack's gym. It was quiet out, as Saturday mornings often were, but he felt an extra eeriness today.

As he walked down the street, he noticed a suspicious looking car parked over the road, far too flash for the usual motors found on his street. The windows were tinted so he couldn't see who the person was in the driving seat.

As his mind danced between paranoia and scepticism having just uncovered what felt like the kind of secret conspiracy plot you'd find in a Hollywood movie, he puzzled over the familiarity of the car. Tommy could have sworn he'd seen it before, a black Mercedes... but at that precise moment he couldn't be sure. Then he saw it as he glanced over his shoulder – the registration – B1 RDS. He knew that registration plate anywhere – Birds Furniture... It was Craig Hargreaves' dad. *What was he doing around here?* Tommy thought anxiously.

Tommy paced on, his mind switching back to the task at hand. He kept his head down and walked quickly past Mr Hargreaves' car, hoping he wouldn't see him. As Tommy reached the corner to turn onto the main road, he heard an engine turn on. He took another quick peak over his shoulder, suspicion getting the better of him. At that point he realised that Mr Hargreaves had edged out of his parking space and appeared to be following him in his car. Tommy spun to face front and walked on, upping his pace to a fast march. As his pace increased, so did the pace of black Mercedes.

Tommy couldn't quite get a handle on what was happening or why, but something inside him told him Mr Hargreaves didn't want to stop for a friendly chat. He'd always felt that Mr Hargreaves disliked him and didn't really know why, he assumed because he was poor and that Mr Hargreaves was a snobby prick. Tommy was starting to think though that this wasn't a coincidence; the morning after a strange man warns him not to ask questions about his dad, Mr Hargreaves turns up creepily following him in his car.

Is Mr Hargreaves linked to this whole situation? He tried to tell himself that it was his mind honing in rapidly on unfounded assumptions; that he was getting the answer 5 from a rather complicated 2+2 – *I mean come on, Craig Hargreaves' dad?* But as he turned onto Glenwood Street and started to jog towards the gym, the black Mercedes made its move and began to increase its speed, seemingly following his every move. He didn't have time to assess the situation any further, it was time to get moving.

Tommy was breathing heavily as his ruck sack began to hop up and down from his shoulders; his strides had extended into almost a sprint now. He heard the noise from the car as the acceleration increased, he frantically looked back and forth over his shoulder. Tommy could see the gym, it was 50 yards away – a safety zone, like his very own embassy whereby if he reached it, he was sure he'd receive diplomatic immunity from any wrong doing by Mr Hargreaves. 30 yards to go. He was panting now and the cold air burned his throat and chest. 20 yards. He could see the black Mercedes out the corner of his eye as he approached the gym, before it edged in front. 10 yards away, nearly there. The car hovered for a split second and then sped off at an almighty pace, its engine noise echoing and bouncing of the neighbouring houses.

Tommy knew that Mr Hargreaves would have seen Brookfield's gym as a no go zone and he was mightily relieved. He was safe – for now. Tommy had no idea what he had got himself into, but he was starting to realise how very real this quest for truth of his could become and he was worried. The early morning dose of adrenalin caused his hands to shake and his legs barely held him up as he stumbled through the door of the gym.

He was greeted by a sight that he didn't expect to see; Councillor Jim Carruthers. Jack was pottering around and tidying up around the gym, it seemed as though they were chatting away and putting the world to rights until the closing of the door behind Tommy interrupted them. They both looked up and smiled. Tommy immediately felt safe and reassured as Cllr Carruthers pleasantly acknowledged him with a friendly wave, before Jack welcomed him with his usual cheek.

"Bloody hell son, have you shit the bed? You're up early for a weekend, aren't you?" Jack said, with a laugh afterwards and a quick look around to see if Cllr Carruthers found him as funny as he clearly found himself – he did. Tommy didn't mind, this is exactly what he needed, some banter and comradery.

"No!" Tommy said forcing a laugh, despite his heart still pounding after his close call on route to the gym, "I didn't sleep too well so wanted to get up and about and couldn't think of anywhere better to go at 9am on a Saturday..."

"Well I must say it's good to see you lad, we need to get some extra training in if we're going to ever get you in that ring – I'm telling you, you're going to be firing for the Granville amateurs in a couple of months' time, we need to get your name down," Jack said, before turning to Cllr Carruthers, "He's a talent this kid you know Jim, mark my words."

"I don't doubt it!" Cllr Carruthers said with a wide smile. "So, how are you Thomas? I must apologise for our last meeting at your school, I must have come across awfully forward when revealing I knew your father, I shouldn't have been so presumptuous"

"Oh I'm ok sir, and please, don't apologise. In fact, it should be me saying thank you to you. Since you mentioned my dad last week, it seems as though the stars have aligned and the universe wants me to find out more about him..." Tommy responded, respectfully.

Both Jack and Cllr Carruthers looked a little puzzled by his revelation and even Tommy himself was a little surprised at how open he was being – *this adrenalin was really something*.

"Actually, I think I'm in a bit of a pickle Jack, that's why I've come to see you... Do you mind if I have a word?" Tommy asked, his question gift wrapped with a great big bow-shaped hint for Cllr Carruthers to give them some privacy.

"Ah don't mind me son, I was just here visiting an old friend, dropping off some charity donations for the kids you know that kind of thing. I've got a celebration coming up too you know, my retirement slash 60th birthday, maybe Jack will bring you as his plus one?" Cllr Carruthers joked as he slowly moved away to allow some space for them to talk.

He was dressed a little more casually today than when Tommy first met him at school. He wore a bright yellow golf polo shirt which unflatteringly hugged his fleshy chest, some tight pants and some shiny slip-on leather shoes. His face was as pink as Tommy remembered, along with his pug nose and sweaty brow. He looked like the typical bloke who would prop up the bar at a working men's club, chatting away to anyone that would listen about how great he was.

"I'll be with you in a minute Jim, don't disappear!" Jack said rather submissively, before turning to Tommy. This notion made Tommy take notice of how important Cllr Carruthers must be, as for the first time he saw Jack appear to be inferior in somebody else's company.

Jack pulled Tommy over to one side by the doorway of his small office – the word office being used loosely. It was a tiny room where Jack housed some of his equipment, such as focus pads, a body belt and other bits of boxing related gear. There was also a small tin where the monies were kept, although Tommy often wondered whether Jack opened his gym for love over money.

"What's the matter Tom, you've got me worried here?" Jack quizzed. It wasn't difficult to see why Jack would be a little perplexed. Tommy wasn't in the habit of coming forward without prompt to say that he had a problem.

Tommy looked around to see Cllr Carruthers on his mobile phone chatting away to somebody that he was clearly familiar with, as he turned away, Tommy felt comfortable enough to open up to Jack about what was on his mind. Jack was all ears as Tommy told him the brief details of the incidents and discoveries over the last week or so and how he'd pieced them together; the photo album and the image of a caring father, the newspaper article documenting his dad's disappearance, the strange man outside of the Junction pub and his warning of stormy waters ahead, the black leather note book with the details of the suspicious deaths of the young people his dad was counselling and or course – the hidden message about Smiler.

Tommy could see that Jack was surprised by his claims and he didn't exactly do a great job in hiding his scepticism. He felt vulnerable as hearing the words out loud made Tommy realise how fictitious his claims sounded. He started to question himself whether he was in fact going crazy.

"I know it sounds ridiculous, Jack." Tommy said, sensing he'd not completely convinced his boxing coach of a conspiracy theory involving his dad, a local drug kingpin and a huge cover up 14 years ago.

"Ridiculous? That's putting it lightly, son." Jack said harshly, before his words softened to a more supportive tone, "I mean, it's not that I don't empathise with you trying to find out where your dad went, blimey, I want to find out where he went! But do you not think this is a bit farfetched? A man in the shadows, conspiracies, cover ups, secret black books - you're starting to sound like he did all those years ago, bloody paranoid!"

Tommy looked away, tears of frustration edged towards the brim of his eye lid. He had to call upon all his might to hold the tears back, but he felt annoyed.

He had come to Jack because he thought he'd understand, yet he wasn't taking him seriously. It was time to show him some proof. Tommy unzipped his bag and pulled out the black book, thrusting it under Jack's nose.

"Don't believe me? Fine! But how do you explain this!" Tommy barked, his increase in volume and animation attracting the attention of Cllr Carruthers, who had finished his call and began to shuffle over slowly, seemingly intrigued by the commotion.

Jack flicked through the book and his expression began to change slightly, but Tommy could see Jack was convincing himself it couldn't possibly be true, Tommy added, softly this time, "Jack, do you not think I know it sounds silly, a script writer for a film would struggle to think it up... but what other conclusion can I draw from this? My dad disappears 14 years ago after becoming suspicious about the deaths of 5 kids who were all linked to one person – Smiler!"

"Smiler?" Cllr Carruthers interrupted, his countenance somewhat bemused now, "Did you just say you think Smiler was behind something?"

"Erm, yes sir," Tommy answered awkwardly, feeling a little embarrassed.

"Ahh, my nemesis! Sorry for ear-wigging, I couldn't help overhear and my intrigue took over... Smiler, Christ, if I had a shilling for every time I'd come across the workings of that nasty piece of work... I've been trying to find out who is behind that alias and clean him off these streets for 30 bloody years, my one failed promise to this town," Cllr Carruthers said, reflecting upon this rivalry, a sense of bitter disappointment coating his words, "I say him – I've never seen him so he could be a she! What's a lad like you doing talking about a piece of work like Smiler?"

Tommy was unsure how to answer this. Did he declare all and risk getting laughed at or keep it to himself and be stuck in the same place with this peculiar mystery? *Cllr Carruthers could be a great person to have in my corner if I decided to go after the truth…*

"Well, it's hard to explain Mr Carruthers… I suppose I'll just come out and say it – I think Smiler had something to do with my Dad's disappearance…" Tommy said apprehensively.

He waited as it felt like an eternity passed. The gym had never felt so quiet, the loud ticking of the clock filled the silence, it could only have been ten seconds, but they were ten long ticks. Carruthers appeared to mull over the statement, before his face began to crack, a smirk crept into a smile which burst uncontrollably into a laugh. Tommy was embarrassed.

"I'm sorry Thomas, I don't mean to ridicule, it's just one of the wildest theories I've ever heard and believe me as a councillor – I've heard some 5-star theories over the years."

Tommy showed Cllr Carruthers the book and explained the back story which has led to his conclusions. Upon seeing the book Cllr Carruthers seemed to take him a little more seriously. Paying extra attention to his dad's notes and seemingly giving them the respect they apparently deserved given that Cllr Carruthers held his father in such high regard.

"Ok Thomas, whilst I still think this is a little farfetched and could well be the scribblings of a man who became a little reclusive and paranoid before he left town, out of my respect for your father and what he tried to do with the young people of this town, I'm going to give you my card with my phone number on. If you want any advice or support around anything, please get in touch. But please, Thomas, I understand you need answers but take it from me - don't go chasing after Smiler, whoever they are, they're a very, very dangerous person with a very, very dangerous organisation, you will either end up in danger or driven barking mad, believe me, I've been chasing Smiler's shadow for decades and when I've gotten even remotely close I haven't been without the odd death threat I'll have you know!"

"Thank you, sir" Tommy said, as Cllr Carruthers placed a comforting hand on his shoulder. He looked down at the card and, despite being laughed at and feeling a little embarrassed, he believed he'd made a very strong step forward by having Councillor Jim Carruthers on side. *They don't have to believe me*.

He was glad he'd restrained from talking about Craig Hargreaves' dad and the car chase on the way to the gym, he wasn't sure whether Cllr Carruthers and Jack could have controlled their laughter if he had suggested that *Mr Hargreaves* was involved in some way as well. Although deep down, Tommy believed that this morning's incident and Mr Hargreaves' sudden interest in him, coming on the back of the man outside the pub, could have no other explanation.

"Right young Tom, are we getting your gloves on today or what?" Jack said, breaking the silence in the gym and switching topic firmly onto boxing.

Cllr Carruthers said goodbye and went on his way. Tommy got changed, laced his gloves up and got a fairly decent training session in, despite his mind distracted by other things. He was worried about what waited for him outside when he left the gym. Furthermore, he was worried about what awaited him as he delved deeper into his father's disappearance and the ugly past of the Granville underground.

CHAPTER EIGHT

The journey back to Frampton Road was a contrast of the journey Tommy had experienced this morning when leaving his house. It had now turned a little cloudy with the drizzle setting in for what looked like the rest of the day. There were a few more people out and about on the streets by this time but the journey was uneventful, despite Tommy feeling on red alert at every person he passed; he even crossed the road when he saw old Mrs Newham reach into her old-lady cart, as he was unsure what she was going to pull out, only to notice over his shoulder that it was simply her small umbrella. Tommy felt tense and wired, his thoughts were bordering on insane. *I need a lie down, man.*

He waltzed through the front door at home and straight upstairs to change his clothes and grab a jacket – he'd already taken advantage of the basic, yet perfectly adequate showering facilities at the gym. He didn't plan on staying long at home to listen to the moans and groans of his mum and brother; hungover, rattling and hostile, once they surfaced from their hibernation. It was almost noon and he sensed it wouldn't be long before they stirred.

As he made his way down the first few stairs, he noticed a big silhouette approaching his house through the stained glass window of the front door. The shadowy figure stopped, turned its head almost 360 degrees, before posting something through the letterbox. The silhouette was dark, shifty with what looked like shaggy hair – very unlike the bright orange fluorescent postman, the whistling bundle of joy who usually posted things through the door at a much earlier time than this.

Tommy sprinted down the remaining stairs, almost falling over himself and grabbed at a small piece of card, which had barely hit the floor. It was rather inconspicuous; probably 2" by 5" in size and it had a handwritten message on it. His eyes widened as he absorbed what was scrawled on the card:

If you want to know more,
Meet me –9th at 9,
I can't tell you the hole truth,
But I know who can

Tommy read it again... he didn't understand it fully but he knew for damn sure what it was related to. Without a second thought, he darted out the front door and onto the street. He turned and looked frantically left, then right and back and forth but there was no sign of the silhouette. It didn't take a genius to work out that it was the bloke from the shadows outside the Junction last night. *What did this guy know? And why on earth was he so cryptic!*

Tommy stared intently back at the business card again, trying to unpick this puzzle or riddle or whatever the hell it was. He started to feel as though he was the victim of some sick joke, that people were teasing him and playing him off against his own paranoia, curiosity and desperation. He tussled internally about whether to go and meet this peculiar person or not. He knew deep down that his curiosity would win, so the real question to figure out would be where in the world he wanted to meet. 9pm was as much as he could draw out at the minute and it was only pure assumption that led him to believe it was 9pm tonight.

A feeling of isolation and despair grew inside of him. He wished he could just go inside and share this burden with his mum and brother, that they could solve this conundrum together. He needed help and despite the only family he had being just a staircase away, he had never felt so alone. He toyed with the idea of telling Derek but he was about as much use as a chocolate fireguard, plus he'd only tell his mum and after the way she reacted yesterday, Tommy reluctantly felt it was the right move to keep them out of it.

He growled in frustration, slammed the front door and stomped off towards the place where he knew he would find a listening ear, some nice food and a chance to figure this thing out.

The drizzle had developed into a heavier rain now and the clouds had shifted to murky grey. Tommy pulled up the collar on his jacket to cover as much of his neck as he could but could still feel the cold rain trickle down his back. He felt as though the weather was a sign. He had a bit of a thing for semiotics and symbolism and he worried that the miserable weather today represented the unfolding mystery he was being drawn into; it also felt much more like the modern day Granville when it was raining – dark, depressing and intimidating – no sign of its sunny and glorious past.

The balance of fear and intrigue was becoming an emotional scrap and Tommy could feel fear beginning to get the upper hand. The thing that scared him the most, currently, was the fact that the man from the shadows knew where he lived.

Tommy was shifty on his travels and his peripheral vision was on high alert for a black Mercedes – he felt like he needed eyes in the back of his head. He got wet whilst walking, but soon arrived unscathed at Kirsten's house. Once that front door opened and he saw her warm, welcoming presence, he realised he wasn't in this alone.

"Hey! Come in... you look soaked!" Kirsten said, opening up her body to allow Tommy to enter into the warmth, "Here, give me your jacket – hang on – 'MUM! Tommy's here can you plate an extra one up for lunch?' – come through, Mum has just made fajitas for lunch." She said, to Tommy's delight – perfect timing yet again.

"Kirsten wait, you won't believe what has happened this morning, I can't even think where to start!" Tommy said energetically before Kirsten had even shut the front door behind him.

Kirsten must have sensed this was juicy information as the animation and enthusiasm was written all over Tommy's face. Tommy followed

Kirsten through to the living room, which was knocked through into a kitchen/diner. Tommy remembered it before the renovation and shared Mrs Cole's view that the home improvements had 'just opened the house right up'. He said hello to Mrs Cole, who responded with a huge smile and a hug, despite just rolling her eyes at Kirsten after she'd asked if they could eat their lunch in her bedroom – clearly Tommy's latest update couldn't wait until after lunch.

"If your dad was here you'd both be sat at that table eating your dinner with napkins tucked in your shirts," Mrs Cole said, already giving in to Kirsten's puppy dog eyes and Tommy, well Tommy didn't even have to do anything to win her over, "but seeing as he isn't, off you go up to your room – but don't make a mess!" She warned, not that it did much good; they were half way up the stairs before she'd finished what she was saying.

Tommy began shovelling his first fajita into his mouth. He always enjoyed the flavoursome food at the Cole residence; it was so tasty and novel compared to what he managed to muster up at home. He imagined this was what it felt like centuries ago when voyagers returned from exotic lands with new spices and flavours and presented them to royalty back home.

"Well?" Kirsten exclaimed. Her eyes were wide with anticipation as she interrupted Tommy from his food daydream, excited for him to spill the beans, so to speak.

Tommy finished his mouthful and then told Kirsten everything; the leather bound book, Smiler, the car chase from Hargreaves' dad, Jack and Cllr

Carruthers laughing at him but then offering him help in the end, then the cryptic note posted through his door by the man from the shadows.

Once Tommy had finished, Kirsten put her plate on the floor beside her bed and for once seemed to be lost for words. Tommy was aware that it was a heck of a lot of information to process; he was still making sense of it himself. Kirsten's look of excitement had faded; her golden brown complexion had turned an unusually pale fawn colour.

"We need to go to the Police."

"Ha! And tell them what? There's more chance of them locking me up for wasting police time, or sectioning me under the Mental Health Act for paranoid delusions." Tommy dismissed Kirsten's suggestion aware of how farfetched this story was; although he really did wish it was an option. He'd certainly feel safer.

"Well, we've got to tell someone! Some freak has found out where you live! Hargreaves' dad is clearly involved-"

"Do you think he's involved with Smiler?" Tommy interrupted.

"Do you not?? You're not telling me selling furniture gets you the house and cars that they've got… Jesus, he's chasing you down in his car Thomas!" Kirsten slammed.

"Woah woah, what are you full naming me for?" Tommy joked, sensing concern in Kirsten's voice. He tickled her belly to tease her in a mild play fighting manner. Kirsten fought back and they rolled around a little on her bed, laughing and playing. In that moment Tommy felt electricity flying through him. He looked at Kirsten and realised that they both felt it. Their eyes locked as Kirsten got the upper hand and pinned Tommy down. The gaze was longer than normal. He'd thought it last night, but wondered if it was the alcohol, he realised at this moment it wasn't. He had feelings for Kirsten.

The line between romance and ungainliness as a 16 year old is a fine one and in true Tommy Dawson style, he slammed the breaks on to a screeching halt and backed up, calling an end to the play fighting and changing the subject back to the puzzling mystery they had in front of them.

"So, erm, what do you make of this riddle then?" He said, awkwardly, pulling out the note again.

"Well... Let's have a think... We know its 9pm and can only assume it means today?" Kirsten said slowly, nestling back on her side of the bed. Tommy noticed her look away slightly, rubbing the back of her neck. She seemed a little flustered and dishevelled and he couldn't tell if she was annoyed or embarrassed. He questioned whether he'd made the right move in stopping the play fighting. *Did she enjoy the flirting too?*

Before Tommy could dwell on that thought, Kirsten continued, "You're not actually thinking of meeting this guy are you?!" She asked, her voice increasing in intensity.

"Course I am! This could be the next clue to finding out once and for all what's happened to my dad..." Tommy responded defiantly.

"Tommy, some old, twisted man is creating riddles for you to solve to lure you to meet him... I've heard some bent-out-of-shape stories in this town but this trumps the lot! You know how dangerous Granville is at night, we hear all kinds of horror stories at school... you could get hurt going out there by yourself!"

Kirsten's manner softened towards the end of her pitch. She was right. There was concern in her eyes as she reached out and gently laid her hand on Tommy's shoulder.

"Well, I was kind of hoping you'd come with me?" he said, sheepishly.

"Oh, I see... you want me to protect you do you?" Kirsten teased, clearly sensing her opportunity for revenge in the wind-up stakes. Tommy laughed, but inside he was genuinely relieved he wouldn't have to brave this alone.

"I'm not sure what use this guy's information is going to be, he doesn't even know the difference between *whole* and *hole..."* Tommy said, making signals with his hands to convey his point.

"Let me see that," Kirsten said assertively, snatching the note from Tommy's grasp. Her eyes danced as she read the note once, twice and then a third time, "I've got it!"

"What? Got What??" Tommy said, alarmed, excited, apprehensive.

"The 9th... hole... - the 9th hole... it's the golf course!" Kirsten declared with an air of smugness, and as she jumped up off the bed to a victory dance.

At that moment, Tommy did something he'd never done before. He leapt to his feet, picked her up and whisked her round in a circle before placing her back on her feet gently. For a quick moment Tommy's excitement had given him an instinctive urge that he wasn't really aware of until after he'd placed Kirsten back down – but it felt good and Kirsten let out her cute laugh as he did it.

"Brilliant Kirsten, absolutely brilliant! We make a good team me and you," Tommy said, buzzing from this revelation.

"Yes, we do!" Kirsten replied, offering that familiar smile that had started to acquire Tommy's attention a little more than usual these last few days.

"Ok, so that's it, 9pm, on the 9th hole of Granville Golf Course... we find out once and for all what this strange bloke knows about my dad – are you with me?" Tommy said with a cheeky grin.

"Of course I'm with you," Kirsten said, "But don't you think it's all a bit spooky and weird, I mean, this guy could murder us or something?"

Tommy laughed a little before noticing Kirsten was genuinely disturbed. "I know, but I've got to take this chance Kirst, it's the only one I've got... Something is telling me that this guy is the key to revealing the whole thing, the truth about Smiler and my dad and what Hargreaves' dad wants with me..." he paused, "...just when I thought I couldn't hate Craig Hargreaves anymore."

Tommy could see Kirsten was troubled and, deep down within, so was he. He tried to put on this brave exterior but his insides were quaking. He tried to reassure Kirsten by putting his arm around her shoulders giving her a squeeze, a sign to let her know it will be ok. He knew she'd follow him to the burning fires of hell, regardless of how scared she was. She was ferociously loyal and that was one of the things he loved most about her.

Tommy flicked the TV on and they settled down to watch the Saturday afternoon film on ITV, which just so happened to be Toy Story. Despite their impending mission to battle to the cold autumn night, go and meet unknown, cryptic characters and try and solve a dark mystery on the volatile streets of Granville, their inner child won them over as soon as they heard the opening theme tune.

As they got comfortable, Tommy found that they were sitting a little closer than usual. They both propped up the pillows behind their backs, necks and head, it was like a cloud of comfort and Tommy felt content. As they made headway into the film, Kirsten nestled her head onto his shoulder and her knee flopped onto his leg. Tommy felt the energy stream through his body, but this time, he managed to keep the awkwardness at bay and go with it. He was tense, but hoped Kirsten wouldn't notice.

CHAPTER NINE

The rain had eased off by 8:15pm, as Tommy and Kirsten prepared to brace the dark night and meet up with the mysterious man from the shadows. They stepped out of the house and closed the door. Suddenly it felt real. The wind was blowing; it felt cool against Tommy's warm face. He was anxious and he could tell Kirsten was too.

They'd passed the time since watching their film by listening to music upstairs and chatting, it came so naturally that they managed to change the conversation from what was going on to more trivial matters – but tonight's task was always there at the back of Tommy's mind. He tried not to let it show to Kirsten, although he suspected she felt the same.

Mrs Cole had fed them both at tea time. Tonight's menu continued the Mexican theme with a homemade chilli, rice, sour cream and this green stuff which Tommy found out off Kirsten afterwards was called guacamole and was made from avocado. In return, Kirsten fed her Mum a story about going to a friend's house and that she wouldn't be too late home but for her to not wait up. Tommy knew Kirsten despised lying to her Mum and he hated to be the cause, it was the one thing she didn't do. Tommy assured her several times that she did not have to do this, but he knew she understood his desire to go and was adamant she wanted to support him. So her only option was to tell a white lie about their whereabouts, as the truth would only have meant Mrs Cole barricading them in the house, or worse still, phoning her dad!

Tommy and his loyal companion made their way up Kirsten's street, across Kirby Lane and through the small park which would cut about 20 minutes off their journey if they were to take the streets all the way around instead. It was a risk, as this park was a hot spot for drinking and drug taking amongst the youth of Granville. The last thing Tommy and Kirsten needed was a fracas with the local dick heads.

Despite its limited facilities – a grassy area where people walked their dogs in the day, a basic play area and a huge brick shelter with benches inside that was nicknamed 'Heaven' by its nightly occupants – the park always attracted a crowd of risk takers, no hopers, drug pushers and vulnerable kids. *Saturday night – brace yourself,* Tommy thought, as they entered the park.

Kirsten linked arms with Tommy as they drew closer to 'Heaven' and the noise levels grew. She had seemed tense already, not really speaking much as they walked and the prospect of facing 'Heaven' must have cranked things up a notch or two. She squeezed Tommy's arm a little – he felt it.

"Don't worry Kirst, we'll sail through here – we probably know most of 'em from school anyway," Tommy said, reassuring himself as much as Kirsten.

The party had already started in 'Heaven'. As they drew nearer Tommy could see that somebody had started a fire in a steel bin. It illuminated the shelter and you could see people bopping around to the music coming from a portable stereo. The graffiti on the inside walls danced in the light provided by the fire. It was actually of a rather high standard, with portraits, 3D graphics and shrines honouring lost souls, not just your usual scruffy street tags, although a customary smiley face was of course present. It was about as cultured and creative as Granville got these days.

There were people downing bottles of spirits, their inhibitions disappearing quicker than the vodka they drank. Boys play fighting, their aggression increasing as the alcohol took hold. People kissing in the corners engulfed in the empty Saturday night romance that drink and ecstasy can generate; boys, girls – it didn't matter to some.

Tommy and Kirsten had to walk past, it was the only way. They edged into the light and shuffled a little quicker than they had been moving. Then he heard it.

"Well if it isn't my mate, Tommy bloody Dawson!" *Craig bloody Hargreaves*.

Tommy and Kirsten turned simultaneously to see Craig standing there with a bottle of cheap vodka, his rat like face animated, arms and eyes wide. He had a cut across the bridge of his nose from Tommy's forehead accidently breaking it a week or so ago.

Hargreaves hadn't mentioned it at school, but now, alcohol and mates in tow, Tommy expected it... with both barrels.

"Craig." Tommy mustered, acknowledging Hargreaves with a nod, his mouth dry and barely able to get the singular word past his lips.

Tommy clenched his fists as he felt the full effects of flight-or-fight kicking in, flight feeling like the favourable option at the moment. He saw that his arrival had got the attention of some of the other party goers, some of them granting him a slight smile of recognition, others with cautious frowns.

"I believe my dad is looking for you..." Hargreaves said in his usual cocky style, cackling with his cronies.

What? Tommy thought, shocked at the unexpected turn on the conversation. *Hargreaves knew his dad was looking for me? ... Did he know why? ... Did he know he was involved with Smiler?* Tommy was bracing himself for a bigger war than he'd first anticipated. Hargreaves continued.

"Good luck when he gets hold of you, *mate!* You're in for a rough ride 'coz he is not happy! Don't worry; I'll make sure I tell him I've seen you." His sarcasm reeked of facetiousness.

And to Tommy's surprise, puzzlement and relief, that was it. Hargreaves laughed, before tipping the remaining contents of his bottle of vodka down his throat. He turned away to re-join the frolics going on inside of 'Heaven', as did everyone else who had taken an interest, although a couple of love birds in the corner hadn't actually come up for breath from their snog-fest to even notice Tommy and Craig's exchange.

Just as Tommy walked off he saw it; a smiley face tattoo on the neck of one of the more senior looking party goers, the iconic symbol of local tyranny. It caught Tommy's attention and he looked up at the person's face, only to be surprised that the man was staring right back, piercing almost. His eyes were locked on Tommy and he felt them burning. The boy – or man rather – was around 20 years old, dark eyes, facial hair and a tidy hair style, the kind which was combed back with an angular line shaved a few centimetres in from the hairline. He almost certainly will have been the source of the 'extracurricular resources' which were being consumed in 'Heaven' tonight. He wore a black hoody with a thick gold chain hanging out over the top. He raised his chin and turned it ever so slightly to give Tommy a clear view of his tattoo – his stare not relinquishing from Tommy's for a split second. He looked menacing and Tommy didn't like being the focus of his attention.

"Come on Tommy, let's go," Kirsten whispered with urgency.

Tommy and Kirsten moved away from 'Heaven'. He took one last look over his shoulder to find the man in the black hoody still scowling at him.

"Smiler must know I know something," Tommy said, panic surfacing, as they paced on into the darkness.

"Well I think Hargreaves' dad chasing you yesterday proves that Tommy!" Kirsten exclaimed, apparently baffled as to why it seemed Tommy was only just realising this now.

"No I know that, but I wasn't 100% sure that it was linked, I thought it was and now after what Craig said it's obvious it was, but I *know* Smiler knows. Did you see him? The lad in the black hoody and the smiley face tattoo on his neck... he was fixated on me like a man possessed. He was letting me know, Kirsten. He was letting me know. I can't believe Craig *knows* about his dad!"

"Well, we don't know what he knows other than that his dad wants to mow you down in his car!" Kirsten said, her attempts at trying to rein Tommy in from panic mode were appreciated but fruitless.

"You're right," Tommy conceded, "I can't think about this right now anyway, we need to focus on meeting up with the bloke from the Junction... What time is it?"

"8:52pm" Kirsten said, after checking her watch. They were cutting it fine and increased their pace on their way up to Granville Golf Course. Tommy was glad of the temporary release of tension following their unscathed bypass of 'Heaven', although he did miss Kirsten's arm linked to his.

The Golf Course looked eerie at night; it was dark and quiet with the October mist hovering over it like a blanket. Tommy and Kirsten had left the light and noise behind them at the club house, which they crept around a few minutes ago. It seemed lively as they peaked through the windows, Saturday night drinking spots usually were in Granville, however now, as they made their way to the 9th tee, the light and noise from the club house was soft and distant. It was 9:01pm and no sign of the man.

"Where is he?" Tommy said, impatiently.

"It's only 9:01pm, maybe we give him a few minutes?" Kirsten replied, "I need a cig man, this is intense!"

"So much for only when you've had a drink, hey?" Tommy joked, rolling his eyes as she rooted in her bag for a lighter. The joke was well timed and shifted the focus away from their meeting with crazy shadow man, even for a split second. Kirsten didn't seem to mind being on the receiving end either. She laughed and stuck her tongue out before lighting her cigarette.

"The *hole*!" Kirsten gasped, exhaling smoke in the process, "Will he not mean to meet at the hole, not the tee?"

"Let's move – quick!" exclaimed Tommy, feeling revitalised by Kirsten's idea. He darted off the tee onto the fairway and Kirsten followed, throwing the remainder of her cigarette and grumbling that she'd had to get rid of it prematurely.

It was wet underfoot but the fairways drained the water well on the course. The 9th hole was a par 4 that turned a corner at a large Oak tree. The flag was currently out of sight. Tommy and Kirsten's eyes had adjusted to the dark and they moved quite well across the grass towards the Oak tree. The tension returned with a vengeance, building with every stride.

They stopped short of the leaning Oak tree, its twisted branches hanging over the edges of the fairway, its trunk thick, wrinkly and aged. Excitement and nerves made Tommy almost tingle – *this was it*.

The wind whistled in their ears like it did in the horror movies, however there was no clichéd wolf cry or token owl; just the sound of their heavy breathing after the quick dash. Tommy and Kirsten looked at one another and gave a nod to signal they were ready. They edged forward and reached the Oak tree, peered round and saw the outline of the flag blowing in the wind. There was a man stood next to it, but he was moving. He was leaving.

"Wait!" Tommy shouted, piercing the quietness. He ran towards to flag at the 9th green giving no regard to the possible risk.

The man stopped and turned. The darkness hid his appearance but it was obvious as they approached that it was the same guy from outside the Junction pub. Tommy and Kirsten reached the flag and stopped about 10 yards short of the man. He looked less scary than the other night, still scruffy, but he looked as though he'd tried to comb his hair, almost like he'd made an effort for their meeting. They were catching their breath when the man spoke.

"Don't come any closer... You're late." He said, sternly.

"Sorry, we got held up... Who are you? And what do you want?" Tommy quizzed, impatiently.

Kirsten put her hand out and placed it on him, indicating that she was concerned perhaps. Now wasn't the time for being polite though, plus the bloke didn't want them any closer; it felt a safer distance and Tommy was more confident that the man wouldn't pounce on them as they'd initially feared.

"I think the question is actually, what do *you* want?" The man said, sticking to his cryptic methods.

"Look man, you clearly know more than I do about this situation, are you getting a kick out of playing with me or something?" Tommy ranted. He was frustrated and irritated. "Because all of this, the note, the mystery, the meeting in secret – it's just weird... I want to know what happened to my dad! I want to know why everything points to Smiler! I want to know who Smiler is! And I want to know who the hell you are!"

"Your dad was murdered, Thomas." The man said bluntly.

It was as soft and subtle as a breeze block landing on Tommy's head from a height. It felt like somebody had punched him in the stomach. Tommy felt numb; however much he'd prepared himself for the high possibility, hearing it knocked him into next week.

"What? How? Erm, when? I mean, I guess I was starting to fear that could be the case... but man, he's really dead?" Tommy mumbled.

"I'm afraid so," The man answered, softer this time, "my apologies for being blunt, but you needed to hear it from the outset, because this path your walking down doesn't lead to flowery gardens, sunshine and reunions with long lost Fathers, if you know what I mean?"

"Go on... I want to know as much as there is to know." Tommy urged.

"Are you sure? Because there's no turning back from this..." The man warned.

"Positive."

"Ok, as long as you know that you're walking into the lion's den... and he's hungry." The man said, one final disclaimer before revealing his information, "You've clearly made the link between Smiler and your father, not bad for a kid... But what you don't know is who and why... Smiler is a ruthless bastard; he'll stop at nothing to maintain his empire and his power over Granville. But he's also a sinister bastard, the real twisted kind. He preys on teenagers, lures them into his world of drugs, sex and crime and abuses them,"

"What do you mean abuses them?" Tommy interrupted; Kirsten's mouth was ajar in disbelief.

"Come on kid, don't be naïve and let's not say more than we have to here, it's hard enough to talk about... I'm talking the whole 9 yards, he entices them, grooms them, gets them hooked on drugs, uses them for his sexual satisfaction and tosses them out into the underworld of Granville to survive the only way they can – drugs and prostitution – which of course suits him because he controls the whole god damn industry. If anyone ever came close to revealing his identity – they were taken care of in the only way he knows how... death."

"Ok, that's heavy..." Tommy said, shaking his head.

"Heavy? It's awful! What a disgusting man... those poor people!" Kirsten exclaimed.

"But what does that have to do with my dad... and how do you know all this?" Tommy enquired, somehow maintaining his focus.

"Your dad stumbled upon a pattern emerging with the kids he supported at work," The man continued, "Kids were disappearing and turning up dead, it's been that way for a long time in this town, few are ever found and justice was rarely on anybody's mind when it came to accidental deaths and suicides – easier to sweep it under the carpet and blame drugs and bad choices than to blame it on a ghost like Smiler. But your dad, ahh your dad, clever as he was, he thought he found the link, the link between the kids, the drugs, the abuse and the deaths or disappearances – Smiler."

"You mean Julia Stark, Brendan Gould and the others?" Tommy interrupted.

"We have ourselves a budding detective here, do we?" The man said, impressed with Tommy's tenacity. "Yes, there were 5 in total, that he knew about. Your dad came to me to tell me, he trusted me with this information and I let him down," The man's voice faded in disappointment.

"But they were a mix of boys and girls?" Kirsten said, confused.

"Gender doesn't matter to a man like Smiler; he's the kind of bloke that gets off on power and fear, different genders just make it more challenging and all the more sweet for him." The man said. Tommy felt a chill through his body.

"Why did he come to you? Who are you?" Tommy pressed.

"Who am I? Ha! I'm nobody, son. But back then I was a policeman and a good one at that. I was fresh out of training and hungry; I was fast tracked to be a D.I. and was making good progress. Me and your dad got to know each other after I let a kid off with a caution on the condition he saw your dad for counselling. We got quite friendly, professionally like. Then he started to become a bit more reserved, was putting the hours in at his office, started asking strange questions and became really shifty and suspicious. One day he approached me and asked for an off the record chat – he had information on Smiler and the deaths of those kids. He believed that whenever one of the kids came close to opening up about who Smiler was, they wound up dead or gone. I thought all my Christmases had come at once – the case of a life time. Ha... like hell it was. I started to collect evidence, poked my nose in a few too many places and bang! I must have pissed the wrong people off because I came in one morning, was dragged into my Sergeant's office, sacked and warned to never speak of anything I'd found relating to this case. They'd already packed my stuff up and left it on the side of the road outside. I lost my job, my house and my wife left me with my unborn child, my world crumbled and never recovered." The man stopped in his tracks and appeared emotional.

"Why didn't you say anything? And what about my dad?" Tommy asked, aware that he needed to be sensitive, but desperate to know more.

"They told me that if I said anything to anyone, my unborn child would never see the light of day. And boy did I believe them... He's 13 now my son, he doesn't even know who I am, if I'd have pushed this case he may never have even been born." A tear on his cheek glistened in the moonlight. He paused for a moment to gather himself before continuing, "I got wind of your dad disappearing; I knew it was a joke the moment I read it in the paper. He'd obviously taken a few steps further into the lion's den than I did. They threatened me and my child and I have no doubt those threats were given to your dad too, the only difference being with him, I think they carried them out in full force."

"This is unbelievable! I knew it! I knew something wasn't right – didn't I Kirsten?" Tommy said, his grief not properly activated and shear excitement and adrenaline taking over. Kirsten looked shell shocked. "What do I do now? I think that Smiler is onto me... Is a man called Hargreaves involved??" Tommy continued to ask questions, but the man began to withdraw upon hearing Smiler was in the know. The man appeared to know all too well that Smiler had eyes and ears everywhere. The years hadn't been kind to him and it seemed this had only fuelled his paranoia and precaution.

"You need to know this could end up really badly for you if you pull at this thread, Thomas," The man warned.

"I know, but he can't get away with this – he killed my dad!" Tommy said defiantly.

"I'm not sure about this Hargreaves fella you refer to, this is the thing, I never actually found out who Smiler was, anyone who gets close ends up 6 feet under. Sorry I can't help you more, but I thought you deserved to know the truth." The man looked down, almost ashamed and began to walk off towards the pitch black night.

"Wait!" Tommy said, "You said in your note, you said you knew who could tell me the whole truth – was that just a gimmick to get me here?"

Tommy felt deflation creeping in, the enormity of the information he'd received was starting resonate.

The man stopped and slowly turned, before responding.

"The kids, the kids your dad was helping..."

"Yeah..." Tommy said, eagerly waiting.

"One was different from the other four..."

"Katie Beardall," Tommy said instantly, her name etched into his mind, "She disappeared, presumed dead but her body was never found!" Tommy said.

The man spoke one last time before he left and vanished into the night.

"She's still alive."

CHAPTER TEN

"Tommy, you can't be serious about not going to the Police now?" Kirsten demanded as she tried eagerly to keep up with him. He marched across the golf course back towards the dimly lit streets of Granville like a man possessed.

"The police? You heard him... The police practically covered this thing up, the abuse, the murders of those kids and the murder of my dad!" Tommy snapped, "Right now I can't trust anyone."

Tommy felt his emotional guard rise to its default position. He saw that Kirsten seemed genuinely concerned and scared. He didn't mean to push her away, he didn't even know why or how his defence mechanism kicked in, it was instinct he assumed.

"You can trust me," she said softly. Tommy forced a smile.

Hearing this stopped him in his tracks for a split second and he managed to pull his thoughts back together from the raging constellation that almost felt external, to a more rational state; the last thing he wanted was to upset Kirsten, especially after the warmth he'd felt in her presence last few days; he just had a hard time shaking off the anger and fear that swamped his whole body.

Tommy and Kirsten walked into the night. It was bitterly cold now, the rain had stopped and the skies cleared to reveal the stars above. Tommy could see the breath in front of his face and it was the first time he'd realised he was cold. They weren't heading anywhere in particular, just walking in almost silence but for the odd car, siren and scream – the soundtrack to a weekend in Granville.

Kirsten had to almost double her steps to keep up with Tommy's intense pace; she'd looked a couple of times as though she wanted to speak but held back. Tommy didn't like the thought of Kirsten treading on egg shells and second guessing herself before she spoke on the count of his sulk; he didn't want to be that guy. He wrestled with his stubbornness before opting to get over himself and break the silence.

"Sorry, I didn't mean to go off on one, Kirst. I guess it's a lot to take in."

"You don't need to apologise, Tom, not after what you've just found out... But thank you."

That still moment which often occurs after an apology hovered for a second. Tommy felt his anger disperse. Kirsten burrowed her nose and chin into her chequered scarf and they continued walking. This cold was really something.

"We need to find Katie Beardall."

"How? Where?" Kirsten said, perplexed.

"I don't know yet, but we need to track her down and find out once and for all who Smiler is. I can't just do nothing; Smiler knows I'm onto him and Hargreaves' dad is going to track me down soon enough on his behalf, which I'm guessing doesn't end too well for me... so, nothing to lose, right?" Tommy said, with a wry smile. He felt his energy and confidence returning.

"You're crazy!" Kirsten said, playfully pushing Tommy's arm.

"Maybe I am!" Tommy teased, softly nudging her right back.

"Let's say we do find her, what makes you think she'll tell us what we need to know?"

"I'm not sure of that either, but I have to try. Maybe if I tell her who my dad is – or was – she might feel a sense of loyalty or injustice or whatever. There's still people going through this horrible stuff now – probably people we know, its sick Kirsten, we *have* to do something." Tommy said with hope.

"Just use your charms," Kirsten said gaily with a spirited laugh that followed. Her face lit up when she laughed, she looked so pretty and it moved Tommy more and more. Tommy chuckled and put his arm around Kirsten. He was so happy to have her by his side throughout this. Without her, he'd have nobody. Or worse still, he'd have to rely on his mum. Then it dawned on him. *What am I going to tell my mum and brother?*

It was 10pm now and after Kirsten suggested calling to see her Uncle and sponging a few drinks before last orders, they arrived at the warm, radiating place that they were both so fond of; the Junction pub.

As they approached the front doors, they swung open violently. Barry, the doorman, was using a punter's head as a battering ram as he launched him out of the pub onto the street. The customer had clearly had a few too many as he landed face first on the pavement.

"That's enough for tonight Wilko', see you tomorrow," Barry said, as Wilko, a regular drinker, part-time scrapper and all round nuisance at the Junction, staggered to his feet and stumbled away down the street, flicking the V's when he was a safe distance away. Barry turned back to the pub, "Evening Kirsten," he said, "just another Saturday night at the Junction."

Kirsten and Tommy laughed and followed Barry inside. Barry was a big burly man and what he lacked in intelligence, he made up for in reliability and loyalty. He was pleasant unlike most doormen; always polite to Kirsten and her family, but if anyone crossed the line in the Junction, he showed them what the pavement tasted like – literally.

It was busy tonight, as Saturday night usually was. A few faces turned to stare at them as they made their way through the busy pub, but on the whole it was a friendly reception from some of the more familiar faces. Barry managed to get Bill's attention and pointed to Kirsten and Tommy as they meandered their way to the bar.

"Bloody hell, you here on your night off as well," Bill joked, "if I'd have known I would have had you in earlier, it's been heaving tonight, few lively ones in."

"Yeah, we just saw Wilko' being sent on his way... Barry is such a sensitive soul when it comes to seeing people out, isn't he?" Kirsten said sarcastically.

"It's what I pay him for, love!" Bill said with a smile, proud of his beefcake doorman keeping the crowd in check, "Now, what are we having?"

"Pint please Bill, if it's ok with you?" Tommy said with the amount of conviction expected from a 16 year old boy, too young to drink, with no money in his pocket. "Although, it'll have to go on my tab, ya see I haven't actually got any money."

"What's new there then?" Bill said, teasing Tommy in the risqué fashion he was renowned for.

"I'll get them!" Kirsten said, relieving Tommy of any more awkwardness and giving her Uncle a warning glare in the process.

"I'm only messing young'un – they're on the house," Bill said, "take a seat if you can find one and I'll have them sent over – usual for you is it, love?"

Kirsten smiled and nodded. Tommy would have been mortified if Kirsten would have had to pay, but she knew Bill would get the drinks in once she had offered to pay, he was old school like that and appreciated those kinds of gestures. Bill liked to look after his own, as long as they knew their manners and didn't take the piss. They found a seat right in the corner, a small round table with two of the small bar stools tucked under it. Perfect.

The two of them chatted away about the evening that had just passed. They drank their drinks and ordered another round before chatting some more. There were lots of eyes and ears in the pub so the volume of their discussions fluctuated depending on what they were saying and who was walking or sitting nearby. Tommy fidgeted with a beer matt excitedly, flipping it and tearing small pieces off until bit by bit the beer matt became a pile of cardboard pieces.

They talked about the man's story, about Smiler and his disgusting abuse, about the murders, about the realisation that Tommy's dad was actually dead and hadn't just ran away, they sat wondering about how many others had suffered the same fate as the 5 children in Tommy's dad's notebook and they sat plotting their next steps, in particular – how on earth were they supposed to find Katie Beardall.

"What about if I ask Bill?" Kirsten asked.

"Ah I don't know Kirst, I don't know whether I want to get people involved in this mess – I've not even told my mum about all this yet," Tommy said cautiously.

"No, I don't mean tell him everything, just ask him about Katie Beardall... There's nobody who sees and hears more about the comings and goings of Granville than Bill, you know what gossips are like after a few beers, you can't shut them up!"

Tommy thought about it for a minute and decided that they had nothing to lose. They waited until kicking out time so the pub was practically empty, the final few being shown the door by Barry, before he put on his flat cap and said good night. The jukebox finished off by playing its final song of the night, the volume turned down now with no crowd to compete with. Janine McAllister was wiping down the tables and putting the chairs up ready for the morning hoover routine by Carol, Bill's girlfriend. Bill was emptying the spill trays of the excess ale which had built up throughout the evening. Kirsten and Tommy propped themselves up by the bar suspiciously.

"How much?" Bill asked bluntly.

"How much, what?" Kirsten responded innocently.

"How much money do you want? You only ever look at me like that when you want something and I'm thinking to myself – what else can she want other than money?"

Kirsten laughed awkwardly, "Well, it's not money we're after... but we do want to ask you something."

Bill, sensing something unusual occurring, stopped what he was doing, whipped his hand towel over his shoulder, rested his elbows on top of two of the pumps and said, "Go on..."

Just as Tommy was about to speak, there was a loud BANG that rattled through the pub. Kirsten and Tommy jumped out of their skin. Tommy felt his heart almost take off out of his body. Bill spoke again, "Jesus Carol! You nearly gave these two a heart attack!"

"Sorry you two, the door was jammed, I was just locking up the front." Carol said flippantly as she waltzed back into the pub to finish her lock down detail.

"Bloody hell you two, you better spit this out, you look like you've seen a ghost!" Bill joked.

Tommy took a deep breath, "Ok, so we were wondering if you knew any information," he paused reluctantly, before continuing, Bill poised with curiosity, "about a girl called Katie Beardall?"

Bill took his time. He looked up and mimed the words 'Katie Beardall' to himself several times as though this was going to prompt his memory recall. His brain was working, Tommy could see that, but as a minute went by he began to lose hope.

"Katie Beardall," Bill finally spoke with more conviction this time, springing Tommy back into life, "that name is very familiar, hang on..." Bill moved towards the end of the bar, "Janine!" he shouted to his barmaid who was busy cleaning up the tables, she stopped and looked up, "Didn't you used to hang around with Katie Beardall?"

"Who wants to know?" Janine said, guarded and defensive like a Pitbull. She was a short girl, in her late twenties Tommy guessed. She had her hair scraped back in a pony that revealed her pale complexion and her tired eyes. She wore a bright red watch, but other than that, she was all in black. She was a plain looking girl, except of course for the scowl she sported at this moment in time. Kirsten knew Janine from working at the pub; she always said she'd found her distant and a little intimidating, the kind of person who only interacted when you needed to. Tommy was hoping she got on with her well enough, as this was looking like a huge turning point in their quest.

"I do, erm did, do... We do." Kirsten said, unconvincingly.

"Why?" Janine said sharply. Tommy sensed their window of opportunity with Janine was not going to be forgiving. He stepped in.

"Hey... Janine is it? I'm Tommy, a friend of Kirsten and Bill, I was just wondering if you could tell me what happened to Katie?"

"Well you can keep on wondering," Janine said with a sting in her voice, "I'll tell you two the same as I told them other folk who came asking questions all those years ago – I don't know anything! ... As far as I know, she's dead!"

Bill had recognised the sensitivity of the issue and made himself scarce in the back, taking Carol with him. Kirsten and Tommy edged their way over towards Janine slowly but surely. Janine tried to squash the incoming inquisition of the two youngsters by continuing with her jobs, wiping the tables and putting the chairs up.

"Janine, I'm Timothy Dawson's son," Tommy said softly, pleading with her. He noticed that she stopped what she was doing when she heard his dad's name, "I've found something, a book of my dad's, it has Katie's name in it. I want to find her so I can talk to her about it... I know she's still alive," Tommy finished, his instincts telling him he'd pushed it too far.

Janine lifted her head; she was facing away from Tommy and Kirsten looking towards the back of the pub. She stared straight ahead for about twenty seconds – it felt like a lifetime.

"She liked your dad," Janine said, still facing the other way. She slowly turned towards Tommy and Kirsten, tears filling her eyes but shear stubbornness and grit preventing them from tumbling onto her cheeks.

Tommy toned it down even more, "Please, if you know anything, I want to try and help her and anyone else who was or still is in her shoes," his sensitive side becoming more and more apparent, surprising even himself.

Janine was appearing a little more emotional now, "Help her? How? She's away from this shithole now so why does she need your help?"

"Ok, well what about all the others who have and will continue to go through what she went through..." Tommy said.

Janine pondered, her eyes darting between the pub door, Kirsten and Tommy, the back of the pub and behind the bar. She looked anxious and indecisive. Tommy wanted to assure her that it was ok, but he didn't want to blow this chance and actually didn't know whether everything would be ok. Kirsten also looked to be holding back a little, which was unusual for her. Janine seemed as though she had a million and one things to say but appeared frightened for who might walk in and hear.

Kirsten then reached out and gently placed her hand on Janine's forearm to reassure her that she was safe. She didn't even have to say anything. It was the most subtle gesture but a gesture packed with maturity, trust and comfort. Tommy picked up on this and noticed the change in Janine's face and eyes, she began to relax a little and you could see the confidence start to build. Tommy was swooning for Kirsten right now, even in this intense situation, he couldn't help it.

"Ok... sit down." Janine said. Tommy and Kirsten pulled down a chair from the table where Janine had previously wiped down and the three of them sat down, leaning in in preparation for what seemed like it was going to be a highly secret and important discussion. Janine had an intense look in her eyes as she readied herself.

"Don't worry, we won't tell anybody anything that you tell us," Tommy said, feeling the need to clarify that before Janine spoke, his heart beating faster by the second.

"You better not!" She said, with an ironic smirk, "Ok, you're right, Katie is alive. Well, I mean she was last time I heard from her, which is a few years ago now. Only she's not called Katie anymore, she changed her name as soon as she ran away from Granville. She lives out of town now."

"We know why she ran away..." Kirsten said softly, encouraging Janine to continue. Janine looked surprised and a little angry.

"You mean that bastard and what he did to her?" she snapped, before continuing in a more solemn tone, staring down at her hands as she flicked a cigarette lighter on and off, on and off, "He's ruined so many lives... He never touched me, I never went near him – I don't even know who he is, she would never tell anyone. The only person she opened up to was your dad. She talked about him all the time you know... 'Oh Tim has helped me so much, Tim's so understanding, Tim this, Tim that'... Ha! We used to tease her saying she fancied him, you know how teenage girls can be. Well anyway, she'd apparently received an anonymous threat, basically saying she would meet a sorry end if she carried on talking to people – obviously meaning your dad – she wouldn't listen though, Tim was the only good thing in her life at that time really."

Tommy was conflicted. Inside he was beaming with pride hearing about his dad, but he was aware he needed to remain empathetic.

"So what happened?" he said.

"She must have started to realise the threats weren't actually empty and disappeared, didn't tell anyone where she was going or when, or who with, we thought the worst had happened, as it happens far too often round here… It was about the same time as, well, you know the thing with your dad in the papers and that," Janine clammed up at this point, perhaps sensing Tommy would be hurting. He remained strong and nodded for Janine to carry on, "Anyway, about 3 months later I get a letter, stamp address from Wrennington, I thought 'who the hells this off?'… it was a letter off somebody called Harriet Barker, referring to herself as my Auntie Harriet and telling me that she was ok and settled down in Wrennington," Janine paused and looked up at Tommy and Kirsten as they clung on to every word, mouths fixed open with astonishment. "I don't have an Auntie Harriet… the letter made reference to stuff only Katie and I would know about… I recognised the handwriting – it was a letter sent in code to let me know she was ok! I was so happy, I cried uncontrollably. I knew why she had to leave and to risk it all to let me know meant the world to me. Anyway, we exchanged letters periodically through the years, but eventually life starts to get in the way and our letters tailed off. Last I knew she was happy, living as Harriet, in Wrennington."

Tommy and Kirsten both looked at each other in amazement. This was unbelievable.

"Thank you, thank you so much Janine," Tommy said, "Is there any chance you have an address for her? I really want to get in touch."

Janine became nervous again; presumably fear was creeping in about the terrible things that could come raining down on her friend if she let this secret out.

"I'm not sure I should… no offence, but this is a secret I have kept for all these years to protect her. If the wrong people get hold of this information…"

"They won't," Tommy and Kirsten said at the same time. This made Janine smile.

"Well if you give me your word, I'll have the address for you next time we're on shift Kirsten," Janine said, "let's just hope she'll want to speak to you… although like I already said, it was a few years ago, she could have moved on." She paused, "So you're doing all this because you found a book?"

Tommy responded elusively, "Something like that."

CHAPTER ELEVEN

The coach door closed and Tommy, closely followed by Kirsten, made his way towards the back to find two empty seats. The weather outside was dull and grey and the rain dashed against the coach windows. The coach was relatively quiet, yet smelt musty as old stagecoaches do, with its purple and blue patterned seats that had speckles of orange and red and a customary cigarette burn or two. If they could talk, the seats would be able to tell all kinds of stories.

It was Saturday morning at 7:20am, Kirsten and Tommy had just purchased a return ticket to Wrennington, a journey south that would take them 4 hours to get there and 4 hours to get back; a journey that they hoped would provide the final piece to the jigsaw which had taken over Tommy's life and tipped it upside down.

They had planned to take this journey throughout the week, their plans relying heavily on Janine providing the address for Katie Beardall – now Harriet Barker. It had been a quiet week in comparison to the roller coaster weekend which occurred prior. Craig Hargreaves was in and out of school with an illness/come-down-from-the-weekend and didn't bother Tommy when he was in. Tommy had managed to escape the clutches of Mr Hargreaves too by mixing up his usual route home, often calling at Kirsten's house for solace.

True to her word, the previous evening whilst on shift at the Junction with Kirsten, Janine had brought to work with her a scrap of paper with the address that Tommy and Kirsten so desired scribbled across it. She reminded Kirsten of the importance of secrecy with this information and hung on a little longer than was comfortable when placing it in Kirsten's hands. And, true to their word, Tommy and Kirsten hadn't said a word to a soul about any of this.

So the two friends found a pair of seats towards the back of the coach where they nestled in for journey. Kirsten had told her Mum she was going out into town with Tommy for the day, failing to mention that the town she was referring to was the other side of the country! Tommy told his mum nothing, feeling there was no need to raise suspicion by pretending his mum would actually be interested in his whereabouts. Kirsten of course provided the snacks for their trip, bottles of pop, crisps and chocolate – the perfect breakfast some teenagers would say. Tommy pulled out his trusty MP3 player and popped an earphone each into his and Kirsten's ears; left ear for him, right ear for Kirsten. Track selection: Half the World Away by Oasis.

The coach bumbled down the slip road towards the motorway leaving Granville behind in its tracks.

Tommy smiled as he gazed out of the window at the passing trees, fields and never ending concrete strip of hard shoulder, for the first time in weeks, he felt himself relax. For the first time in his life, he was leaving Granville. The coach gained in speed and ticked along nicely in the slow lane. Before they knew it, Granville was out of sight and almost out of mind.

Three and a half hours of travelling, a stop at the service station for a pee, a 45 minute walk from the Wrennington bus station and a few wrong turns later, Tommy and Kirsten stood facing 79 Ashley Avenue, the last known home of Katie Beardall aka Harriet Barker. It was a leafy, old fashioned avenue, with trees on either side of the road, grass verges, wide pavements and a road that could fit two buses down it.

The house appeared rather grand compared to what they were used to in the slums of Granville. It was semi-detached with a huge driveway; the front garden would have been considered a park back home. Tommy felt way out of place, for obvious reasons. This was the kind of house he could only dream of.

"She's done well for herself," he said, rather surprised by the residence of the former Granville runaway.

Kirsten looked in awe, "Tell me about it! I'd love to live here; it's like something off a TV show."

The two friends confirmed the plot which they had conjured up on the way down here – Tommy to knock on the door and introduce himself, explain a little bit about his dad, the book, Kirsten to stand by his side looking friendly, with all her fingers and toes crossed just hoping that Katie – or Harriet – makes a connection with their intentions and agrees to help.

"Worst case scenario – she tells us to do one and we've wasted our time," Tommy said boldly attempting a nothing-ventured-nothing-gained persona, "at least we got out of Granville for the day."

They made their move, crossing the street towards the driveway of number 79. Tommy's adrenalin was on turbo – he was super nervous, excited and scared all rolled in to one big basket of butterflies which whizzed around his tummy. They entered the driveway, Tommy's legs started to turn to jelly and the words - *What am I actually doing?* – bounced all around inside his head.

Tommy reached the door first; it was a huge, wooden, double door, with stained glass windows which gave a blurry view of what was inside – another door. He took a deep breath and knocked with three polite, consistent knocks. Tommy held his breath as they waited.

There was life inside the house as the porch door opened and a figure appeared through the stained glass, trying to shoo a dog inside by the sounds of it. The figure closed the porch door behind them, unlocked the latch and opened one of the front double doors. It was a young woman, late twenties or early thirties, Tommy couldn't be sure. She looked slightly stunned by the two unfamiliar faces of Tommy and Kirsten that greeted her. *Could this be her?*

"Oh! Hello... Can I help you?" The woman said, a confused look upon her face as she folded her arms and leant on the other door which remained closed. She was a pretty woman with a pale but clear complexion. Her dark hair was tied up with a fringe that brushed the top of her eyebrows. She wore an untucked white shirt with maroon stripes, the sleeves rolled up to her elbows. The shirt was baggy, hanging off her slight frame.

"Hi," said Tommy, his voice shaking a little with nerves, "We were hoping to speak to Harriet Barker?"

"Yes, that's me... What do you want?" The woman responded, her confusion increasing quickly as her patience did the opposite. She began to fiddle with an earring and became a little nervy.

Holy shit! Tommy thought, taking a quick glance at Kirsten who seemed equally as overwhelmed.

"Erm, well, this is going to sound a little crazy," Tommy said, "My name is Tommy Dawson, I am the son of Timothy Dawson..." he paused, noticing Harriet's eyes widen like saucers despite her trying to hold a neutral face, "Do you remember my dad?"

Harriet looked around outside the house, down the driveway, up and over the front garden bushes. She was on edge.

"Look mate, I don't know what you want but you came to the wrong house, ok?" She growled between her grit teeth. It was clear she was torn between wanting to stay quiet and not make a scene, but also wanting to let Tommy and Kirsten know she was seriously pissed off with their intrusion on her new life. He got the message, loud and clear.

"We don't want any trouble, I promise... just 5 minutes of your time, please! I've just got a couple of things to ask you, please..." he pleaded, "We've come down from Granville, I don't know who else to go to, you know what it's like back home, its horrific, there's kids still going missing, maybe being murdered, I've just found out my dad was killed and that seems to have put me right in the thick of it... I know you had it rough too... please, just a few minutes and we'll be gone out of your life for good, I promise."

Tommy had planned on playing it a little cooler than this, but he sensed he may only have one chance, so he went hell for leather and the words just seemed to pour out of his mouth.

Harriet looked up and down and all around the street again, "Did anyone follow you here?" she said, looking Tommy and Kirsten dead in the eyes.

"What? No, of course not... nobody knows we've come here, I promise," Kirsten said innocently.

"Well I can't wait to hear how you found me then! Jesus bloody Christ I can't believe this... you better come in!" Harriet conceded.

She must have been wondering what on earth she'd done to drag this old ghost back from the depths of her past. She moved aside to show Tommy and Kirsten into the house, took one last peak outside before closing the door behind them. "My husband's due home in an hour... I suppose you'll want a brew after travelling all this way?" Her sarcastic tone put Tommy and Kirsten at ease a little. They gave their brew orders; Tommy tea with one sugar and a dash of milk, Kirsten a milky coffee with two sugars.

They settled down at the kitchen table with their hot drinks. The house was well decorated on the inside, simple, new and modern, nothing too fancy but well maintained and clean. There was a framed picture on the chest of drawers of Harriet, a man and a child who was no more than 6; Tommy saw Kirsten smile as she picked it up and took a closer look. The fridge was full of kids painting's and there were toys neatly stored in the corner alcove of the back room. *Harriet had a daughter.*

Whilst the kettle was boiling Tommy and Kirsten between them had told Harriet about asking Janine for her address and some of the events which had led up to that, such as the book that Tommy had found in his attic, the car chase and stalking by Mr. Hargreaves and the ex-policeman from the shadows who had told them that she was still alive.

"So... I'm guessing you haven't come all this way just to tell me this?" Harriet said with a conservative grin.

"Well, no... I want to know more about Smiler..." Tommy said. Harriet's face became uncomfortable and her body visibly squirmed at the sound of his name, "You see, in this book of my dad's it had your name – erm, your old name – and a few others and one thing linked them... Smiler... then the old copper told us what Smiler did to people and what he did if they ever told anyone and then he told me that Smiler had my dad killed and well, I want him to pay!"

Harriet managed to gather her focus enough to speak although her eyes were still glazed over, "Yes and that just sounds so heroic doesn't it? Do you know what a man like Smiler does to teenagers like you? Like me, when I was probably even younger than you..."

Tommy and Kirsten sat back in their chairs and listened as Harriet launched into her story, about the lure of drugs and alcohol and how attractive it was to her rebellious teen self, hanging out with older teens and adults who tricked her into thinking they cared about her and respected her. She told them how at the start it was fun and different, but the drugs and the alcohol became heavier and with that came reckless choices.

She told them how Smiler selected her to attend private parties. She was confused by Smiler's power, believing it to be affection when really it was all a sick, twisted plot to abuse her; emotionally, physically and sexually. She knew that she wasn't the only one, but felt so ashamed and scared that she couldn't tell a soul.

"I was so stupid!" Harriet said, shaking her head, tears beginning to fall down her cheeks.

"No!" Kirsten snapped, sounding equally as emotional, "No you weren't stupid! You were young and impressionable and a sick, devious bastard took advantage of you – don't you dare blame yourself!"

Harriet gave a cynical nod, "I wish I had your feistiness when I was your age, I could have done with it... Well, there you have it, he duped me good and proper, once he'd had enough of me, he beat me up a few times, threatened me, my family, threatened to tell everyone I knew that I was a little slag if I didn't do exactly as he said, when he said it..."

Tommy and Kirsten were desperate to hear more but allowed Harriet to do it in her own time;

Tommy was trying really hard to listen to every word she was saying, not wanting to be distracted by the killer question that was perched on the end of his tongue ready for launch; *who is Smiler?*

She continued, "I was so scared, I still have nightmares now. I didn't know where to turn, my family thought I was a little druggy, school weren't interested and I was exactly where he wanted me, lonely, isolated and petrified. Then your dad came along, bless him, he was a lovely man, he really understood me, ya know? He didn't judge me, I'd finally found somebody I trusted and felt I could start dealing with the shit going on in my life. That was up until the death threats. I thought it was just the usual threats from that bastard and the goons that work for him, but they became more intense and real. People I knew were found dead and I thought – I need to go, leave, right now, or I'll end up exactly like that... dead..."

One single tear fell from Harriet's eye; it caressed her cheek all the way to the corner of her mouth, where it hung for a split second before making its way to her chin and falling.

Harriet zoned out for a second but came back in the room to finish her piece, "I'm sorry about your dad, Tommy."

Kirsten hugged her cup of coffee, allowing time for the dust to settle. She cleared her throat and that broke the silence before she spoke.

"Harriet, I just want you to know that I think you're so brave and I'm sorry for what happened to you," Kirsten looked like she was about to cry as empathetic tears appeared in her eyes. Harriet nodded, offered a heartfelt acknowledgement and reached out to squeeze Kirsten's hand.

It was very emotional and Tommy thought about leaving it there, he loathed the prospect of dragging Harriet back even further into her miserable past, when she had already, unmistakably, relived so much pain and suffering in the last few minutes. But he was still without the answers he really wanted or needed. If he walked away from the situation having not pushed it as much as he could he knew he'd regret it and more importantly, he'd be back to square one in terms of finding out who Smiler is and how to avenge his father's murder. He couldn't just leave it, not now he was within touching distance.

"Harriet, what happened to you is absolutely awful, nobody should have to go through that. But, you survived!" he said. Kirsten and Harriet both shot deathly looks at him and he soon realised he'd perhaps stepped a little further away from the sensitive model he was planning on. He continued, "What I mean is, you got away and made a life for yourself, so many others didn't and will continue to meet the same demise unless something is done."

"What do you want from me, Tommy?!" Harriet despaired.

"I want you to tell me who Smiler is so we can end this thing once and for all!"

As soon as the words left his mouth he realised the enormity of what he was asking. Tommy felt awful pushing it like this. He could see how difficult Harriet had found it to open up and here he was, asking her to dig deeper inside her vulnerable soul and tell him, a total stranger, what was there.

His pulse was through the roof as he waited, time seemed to pause and the muscles all over his body tingled in anticipation. This was it, the moment of truth.

"You don't understand, he's so dangerous... I can't do it, I just can't, he'll find me and he'll come after you like he has the rest of us... walk away Tommy, just walk away," Harriet pleaded.

Tommy stood up becoming animated, "Harriet, please trust me! I'm in too deep already, I need to do something... it can't go on! I can't avoid Hargreaves' dad forever, he's going to get hold of me whether I like it or not! I know people who can help, the ex-copper might know people, Kirsten's Mum and dad are good folks, I have a contact in Granville, a really well placed contact, a councillor called Jim Carruthers, he's offered to help us any way he can, I've even got his card, he's been after Smiler for years..."

Harriet's face dropped to the floor as if she'd seen a ghost, her eyes were stone dead, her mouth struggling to speak, "You just don't get it do you?" She hesitated, "Carruthers *is* Smiler."

Tommy slumped back in his chair, his whole body became numb as images and thoughts chased each other around his mind. He had visions of Carruthers; all the sleazy moments which he'd overlooked seemed so glaring now. The way he looked, the way he moved; it seemed so obvious. *A man in power. A man with connections. A man who knows Granville like the back of his dirty, blood stained hands.*

Kirsten too appeared to be in shock and disbelief, but her initial concern seemed to be Tommy. She rubbed his shoulder comfortingly, but didn't offer any words that could fill the silence and soften this scandalous revelation. Finally, after a few minutes, Tommy found it within him to speak.

"I can't believe it." He said, devastated. He felt so foolish and embarrassed.

"You weren't to know," said Harriet, "he's tricked a lot of people, Tommy."

"Well he's not going to get away with it!" Tommy stamped defiantly.

"You're not going to let this go are you?" Kirsten resigned, "I mean, I'd try and convince you that it's too dangerous, you could get killed etc. etc., but knowing you like I do, I know there's no point," Tommy looked up at Kirsten before she declared, "So, I guess what I'm saying is, I'm with you, wherever this goes, I'm with you."

Tommy reached out and grasped Kirsten's hand. He smiled and felt slightly more reassured, which in percentage terms took him to around 1% reassured and 99% petrified.

"I hate to break up the love affair guys, but my husband is due home any minute and whilst I'd love nothing more to introduce him to my troubled past, I'm kind of thinking it's best for everyone if we pretend this visit never happened." Harriet was about as subtle as a sledgehammer. She was up out of her chair and showing Kirsten and Tommy out of the back room into the hall when she stopped and spoke again.

"Before you go, I want you to know I don't take any pleasure in sending you back off to Granville to face that monster, but you have to understand that nobody can ever find out where I am, not just for me, for my daughter," she looked over at another picture of family happiness framed on the wall, "If I thought you'd listen, I'd try and convince you to never return to that horrible place and live happily ever after... but you don't strike me as the type to run away from your problems, however huge they are!"

Tommy appreciated Harriet's stance, he smiled and nodded to let her know it was ok.

"Thanks for trusting us," Kirsten said, flinging her arms around Harriet rather forwardly.

Harriet managed to escape Kirsten's overly friendly clutches and said, "I wish you all the luck in the world you two, you're going to need it! But seriously, you're about to take on Satan himself, you know, when you dance with the devil, he's not the kind of guy that lets you sit down before his song has finished, if you know what I mean." She paused, "Stay safe you two, Granville needs you."

"Thank you." Tommy said, as they exited the double front door of the fancy semi-detached in Wrennington and began their journey back towards the gates of hell.

CHAPTER TWELVE

"So, what are we going to do?" Kirsten asked, rather flippantly given the circumstances. Her question would be more suited to figuring out Saturday night plans, not bringing down a high powered drug king pin, with the law in his pocket and decades of murder and manipulation under his belt.

The coach was bundling along the final stretch of motorway towards Granville, after a long and solemn journey. There was a metaphoric and literal black cloud above the town in the distance. Bad weather was coming and that wasn't all.

"I need to tell my brother," Tommy said, "He needs to know that Dad didn't just leave, that he was a good man, trying to do a good thing. This whole business with my dad has shaped Derek's life for the worse; he deserves to know the truth... I just hope it doesn't send him over the edge - he struggles coping with the news his doctor's appointment has been changed, never mind that his dad, who he believes abandoned him, was in fact murdered."

Kirsten nodded, "What about your mum?"

"I've not decided yet. This is the sort of thing she could really lose her shit over you know? That's if she believed me."

"And Carruthers? I know you haven't got all the answers Tom, but I'm going to be straight with you, I'm petrified. If a man in such a trusted position can reign terror over a whole town, the town he's supposed to protect and nobody be able to stop him for 30 years... what on earth are we going to able to do?"

Tommy clenched his teeth together and tightened his jaw, swallowing hard. He felt scared too, the fear engulfed him. "I'm not sure Kirst; I've played most of my hand by showing Carruthers the black book. He knows I know about Smiler being linked to my dad, so it's only a matter of time before he tries to silence me."

Kirsten appeared deep in thought for a second or two.

"One thing in our favour though Tom, Carruthers doesn't know that we know it's him, yet," said Kirsten.

"He's not getting away with it this time, whatever I have to do, I'll do."

The rain began to fall and within seconds it was hammering the windows of the coach as it pulled onto the slip road and made its way into the outskirts of Granville. They were home and the biggest challenge of Tommy's life awaited him.

It was 6:10pm as Kirsten and Tommy opened the door to Tommy's house. Tommy didn't bring Kirsten round here that often, so as he turned the key, he closed his eyes and hoped for the best. As usual the house wasn't particularly warm, but more unusually, it was a little tidier than expected. His mum was pottering around between the living room and the kitchen, she was half cut but Tommy sensed it was the good kind given the state of the house and the smile she greeted them with. If the half empty bottle of vodka on the fireplace didn't give it away, the slurring sure did.

"Thomas! Kirsten! What do we owe the pleasure?" Theresa said, her sarcasm subtle but still lingering, "Kirsten love, long time no see, how's things on the nice side of town?"

She couldn't help but show contempt towards anyone who managed to be doing ok in life, but disguised it well enough with a hug, just about managing to avoid Kirsten's hair with the built up ash at the end of the cigarette trapped between her fingers. The ash curved, longing to be flicked off into an ashtray where it belonged.

"Alright Mum, is Derek in? And if so is he in a fit state?" Tommy asked, trying his hardest to appear casual and hide the turmoil inside of him, he had pain in his eyes though and any sober, attentive mother would have seen it, but not Theresa.

"Ooh why do you always have to put us down Tommy, especially in front of our guest?" his Mum said, swaying a little as she emphasised the word guest and pointed towards Kirsten, "he's upstairs getting changed, although he's been up there a while so heck knows what he's been up to – actually don't answer that!" she burst out laughing before finishing, nudging Kirsten, "boys will be boys hey!"

His mum had no idea how inappropriate she had just been as she toddled off back into the kitchen; Kirsten looked uncomfortable, presumably visualising the image of Derek that his mum had kindly created.

"Eww – what the hell?" Kirsten whispered to Tommy.

"Welcome to my life! Come on, let's go upstairs – don't worry, you can wait in my room."

Tommy turned and led the way up the narrow stair case which was encased on either side, making it dark and dingy and almost tunnel-like. Tommy was trying to focus on the task ahead but he was feeling self-conscious and couldn't help wonder how Kirsten was finding the experience inside his house. His mum was so unpredictable, it put even him on edge, never mind somebody as sweet and caring as Kirsten.

There was a blatant gulf between their social statuses; it was the unspoken difference between them as friends and Tommy knew that she'd always taken extra care to make sure it never became an issue. Kirsten didn't ever proclaim to be posh, or even from financial advantage and was vocal about her dismay towards those people that made it their business to look down on others. Today however, right here, right now, it was very apparent of just how privileged she was in terms of her stable family, her selfless parents and her clean and tidy home and just how unprivileged Tommy was in those stakes.

Following his extra loud knock on Derek's bedroom door, Tommy slipped inside to find Derek having an innocent snooze on his bed and nothing untoward going on, as was suggested could be the case by his mum. After a few clicks of his fingers, a glass of water and a splash to the face, Derek came round to a semi-sane state and the two of them joined Kirsten in Tommy's bedroom.

"Sit down Derek, I've got something to tell you," Tommy said, still with no idea of how he was going to explain what he had to tell his brother.

"Woah, this is all a bit serious isn't it?" Derek said, temporarily smiling. He cut the smile short noticing it wasn't reciprocated and Tommy instead looked stern and on edge. Derek became uneasy, a position he never particularly enjoyed.

"I've found out some stuff mate, some really big stuff which is going to turn your world upside down... It's about Dad," Tommy began.

"Go on," Derek said. Tommy felt a clang of anxiousness yo-yoing from belly to throat and back again and he imagined Derek felt the same.

"I know what happened to him..."

A big smile appeared on Derek's face; almost as if he'd morphed back into his former 9 year old self, a time when he was happy, before the heroin and the heartache. This was even harder than Tommy had thought it was going to be, he hated to be the one to dash that hope and joy in his brother's face.

"No, no Derek, it's not good, it's the opposite in fact... He's dead," Derek's face fell instantly and he looked down towards his lap – the modern day Derek had returned, "He was murdered Derek, murdered in cold blood – by Smiler! Dad had cottoned on to his secrets and was trying to expose him!" Tommy exclaimed.

Derek lifted his head to look at Tommy and Kirsten, a surprising smirk across his face, "Jeez Tom, what's brought this on? I thought I was bad for making stories up about dad, but this tops the lot!"

"It's true!" Kirsten enthusiastically interjected, typically jumping to the defence of her friend. Derek looked puzzled.

Both Kirsten and Tommy started from the beginning and brought Derek up to speed with everything they knew. They revealed that Katie Beardall was still alive and told him everything she'd said, leaving out the specific details of her new identity as promised. They told him about Mr Hargreaves hunting him down, the old Policeman from the shadows, the black book, the missing kids, the fact it all linked to Smiler who was, according to Katie, actually Cllr Jim Carruthers and that his dad paid the ultimate price for trying to bring him down.

"That councillor bloke?!" Derek said, shocked to the core, "Man oh man, this is bananas Tom, it really is, I can't deal with this right now," Derek was beginning to panic as the enormity of the information registered, his eyes darting, his mind frantic, "I need to tell Mum."

Derek's instinct to turn straight to his mum typified their relationship, mainly as they were each other's emotional crutch, but also, in this case probably more significantly, because they shared the same coping mechanism – drugs. It was a coping mechanism lodged so firmly in the vaults of their subconscious minds that they were incapable of responding to problems in any other way. It wasn't even about the effects of drugs as such, after all these years they'd diluted somewhat, it was what they represented – an escape. The choice between dealing with a difficult situation or the promise of instant gratification from their overworked dopamine circuit was quite literally a no brainer.

"You can't!" Tommy pleaded, "Remember how insane she went the last time I mentioned Carruthers' name and that was without the claims of murder, child abuse and drug trafficking!"

Just then, Tommy's phone beeped as he received a text message. He didn't receive many and the ones he did get were usually from the people in the room with him right now. In keeping with everything else materialistic in Tommy's life, his phone was old, basic and second hand, but it did the job and allowed him to receive text messages and phone calls and occasionally send messages of his own when he mustered enough money to get some credit.

"Text message, from Jack," Tommy said as he pushed the buttons on his Nokia, before reading the text message out loud, slowly, "Come to the gym son, I need to see you," Tommy looked bemused, "That's weird, Jack isn't normally at the gym at this time on a Saturday and he never sends me a text, it must be important."

"Well, let's go and see him," Kirsten said, offering Tommy a look that suggested she would feel more comfortable if they left Derek on his own to process the bombshell they'd just dropped on him, instead of them just staring at him in the close confines of Tommy's bedroom.

"Derek, we'll be back soon to talk about this and what we're going to do about it – don't tell Mum! And for once, please don't go and get spangled!"

Tommy knew the second request was a long shot but he really hoped Derek took note of the first one. His mum can't find out about this, not yet, she could blow the whole thing.

Tommy and Kirsten left Derek sat on the bed staring into space and headed out, back into the wind and the rain to make their way to Brookfield's Gym to see Jack. The sky was dark and opaque with thick, black clouds tussling with the moonlight. The rain shot down and soaked them as they pondered over what Jack would need him for. In keeping with the last few days, Tommy kept one eye looking over his shoulder.

The pair held hands as they walked, more out of security than intimacy but neither of them complained and Tommy actually quite liked the excuse to make physical contact again, to get his fix of that slight electricity that he'd become so fond of recently.

"Do you think Jack knows about Carruthers?" Kirsten asked with tautness in her voice.

"Jack? No way! He's a good man, there's no way he'd have known about any of this and kept quiet," Tommy paused, "I mean I think that's right, but I suppose given everything what's come to light you never really know, do you?"

"I'm sure it's nothing to do with that anyway, he probably wants to talk about boxing for a change," Kirsten said rolling her eyes and pretending to fall asleep towards the end of her sentence, indicating her sarcastic delight at the prospect of listening to Jack and Tommy discuss boxing, not for the first time. The joke made Tommy giggle and he felt reassured.

She had a cracking sense of humour and it was always so well timed.

He was looking at things through a completely different lens lately, what he once saw as joking around between friends, now seemed to have all the signs of flirting. It certainly felt like it, although he couldn't be sure. *Does she feel the same way?*

He squeezed Kirsten's hand a little tighter as they continued the short journey to Glenwood Street and Brookfield's Boxing Gym, passing several of the iconic smiley faces sprayed across the walls; a symbol that now meant so much more to him than ever before.

CHAPTER THIRTEEN

They arrived at Brookfield's Boxing Gym in no time. Unusually, it was dimly lit with only the wall lights turned on, which gave off a bit of a creepy vibe and a sense that it was closed. In the week, whilst evening classes were going on, the place was illuminated, a beacon of hope, determination and positivity, full of hustle and bustle amidst an otherwise destitute community. But tonight the gym seemed consistent with the rest of the town's architecture; worn out, desolate and uninviting. The door was ajar. Tommy glanced at Kirsten, he felt uneasy as he walked in, closely followed by Kirsten.

"Jack!" Tommy called.

"Through here, son," Jack responded.

Tommy and Kirsten walked through to the punch bag area, where the lockers were and Jack's small office. Jack was sat perched on one of the old, cast iron radiators, "Oh! Hello Kirsten, I didn't expect to see you..." Jack said, with a rather uneasy, forced smile.

Jack didn't look his usual perky self. He walked over to one of the lockers and opened it with his own key. Jack reached inside towards the back and pulled out a secret bottle of whiskey and a glass.

"Everything ok, Jack?" Tommy asked, sensing that all wasn't as it should be; gym in near darkness, Jack in a sombre mood and now reaching for whiskey.

"Yeah, yeah, everything is fine Tom. I just asked you here as I've not seen you all week and you know, I thought I'd check in and see how you were?" Jack poured himself a whiskey into the small tumbler glass as he spoke, his hand with a slight tremble. He seemed a little shifty. Something definitely wasn't right.

Tommy swallowed nervously, "To be honest Jack, I've been better, had a bit of a whirlwind few weeks, but, are you alright? You seem a little... off?"

"I'm fine son, just a bit of a bad day that's all. Go on tell me what's been going on, I'm all ears," Jack said, encouraging Tommy to share what was on his mind. He seemed to settle down a little once he'd taken a gulp of his scotch. Jack had never done anything for Tommy to ever doubt him and if he said he'd had a bad day, he'd had a bad day.

"Well, I've found out what happened to my dad. The book I found, it led me to some people who told me what I needed to know... He was killed, Jack! By Smiler!" Tommy cried.

"Not this again Tom, I thought you were going to let this drop–"

"Smiler is Jim Carruthers, Jack!" Tommy interrupted and Jack's face sank, "Jim Carruthers killed my dad because he was about to expose him for exactly what he is, a dirty, abusive, murdering bastard!"

Jack looked as though he was trying to remain composed but Tommy could see he was on edge, it was visible now, "Look Tom, these stories about black books, secret meetings and Jim Carruthers murdering your dad under the pier are starting to sound like something out of a story book, you're starting to sound crazy..."

Tommy was about to interrupt and respond, before he stopped. His brain took a second to catch up as Jack continued to talk. Tommy could hear the sound of Jack's voice but it was muffled, his brain was latched onto something else, something Jack had just said. Then it dawned on him.

"I never said anything about him being killed under the pier..." Tommy said, backing away, protecting Kirsten and looking at Jack with a mixture of disbelief and denial, "Jack? Please! Please tell me you aren't involved in this as well?"

Before Jack could answer, his office door opened and out walked Jim Carruthers followed by three of his goons. Carruthers was dressed in a smart tweed suit, a pink shirt which matched his complexion and a shiny white tie. He was looking mighty pleased with himself.

His goons were mean looking men, big, strong, smiley face tattoos on their necks as standard and giving off an aura that they were capable of unspeakable things upon orders. Tommy recognised one of them straight away, the one with the goatee beard. It was the man who forced his way into his house and pinned his mum up against the door a couple of weeks ago. Kirsten gasped as her hands covered her mouth in shock. Tommy's heart sank to depths he'd never felt.

"Quite a story you've got yourself there, Thomas," Carruthers said, cold and calm, unflustered by the prospect of being exposed, like a man in complete control. Jack looked guilty and ashamed. "You've been a busy boy I see. And of course you have proof to support your claims?" Carruthers continued, "and back up? Please tell me you have people to help you bring down the almighty Smiler?" He laughed, turning to his goons who chuckled with delight and ridicule.

"You're not going to get away with this, you Bastard!" Tommy screamed, edging forward slightly but sensing it may be wise to back off.

Any path towards the door was now blocked by Carruthers' men as they circled Tommy and Kirsten like vultures. They were trapped.

"Oh you see but I am," Carruthers taunted, "just like I have all these years. That's right, you came here thanks to a little help from my good old friend here Mr. Brookfield, nobody knows you're here because the only people who are supposed to care about you are dead, have betrayed you," he glanced at Jack with pity, "or are probably lying face down in a puddle of their own saliva after another pathetic hit just to get them through another couple of hours of their pathetic lives!"

Carruthers' voice reached a crescendo. He was snarling now, enjoying the moment, parading the floor like this was some kind of performance and those in the room were the crowd. He moved over towards Kirsten, stepping inside her personal space. She recoiled with discomfort as he held himself just a centimetre or two from her face.

"Ooh you are a very pretty thing aren't you," Carruthers said. He turned to look at Tommy, "I can see why you're joined at the hip, she's insatiable," Kirsten spat in Carruthers' face. He laughed it off, barely even flinching. He pulled out a cotton handkerchief from his pocket and wiped himself down before adding, "It's a shame you're a year or so too old for me... tie them up!" he barked, his assailants immediately responding and making a move towards Kirsten and Tommy.

Suddenly Jack burst in to life, "You said you wouldn't hurt him! You said you only wanted to talk to him!" he pleaded with Carruthers.

"And him!" Carruthers ordered; his words as frosty as his heart, "He's no good to me now."

Tommy could see the man who had threatened his mum much clearer, now he wasn't half a flight of stairs away. He had one blue eye and one grey eye and peculiar looking eyebrows that were thin and sculpted, matching his goatee beard. He made light work of restraining Kirsten; twisting her arms painfully behind her back and tying them with plastic tie wraps as she yelped in pain and panic. It hurt Tommy that he couldn't do anything to protect her.

The second of Carruthers' men was a large, ugly looking bloke. He wore a leather jacket, had huge bulging eyes and a chubby face. The blood vessels on his nose were almost purple. He gripped Jack in a bear hug, squeezing the old man until the life drained from his face before tying him up as his commander instructed.

The third of Carruthers' goons was a little smaller than the second and was slow to react, giving Tommy an advantage and making him a little bit more difficult to apprehend; they tussled and fought, Tommy determined and feisty as he managed to land a swift left hook to the jaw of the third man, which wobbled him. It was futile though as one swift blow to the back of the head from Carruthers with an expandable cosh ended the struggle and put Tommy to sleep. Lights out.

When Tommy came round from his unconscious state, the first thing he noticed was that he had a splitting headache. It was pounding, the source of the pain sitting at the back of his skull. As he awoke, the events which preceded came rushing back to him and he snapped back into life, only this time, he couldn't move his arms or legs as he was bound to a chair. He looked around him to realise he was tied to a wooden chair, which sat in the middle of one of the boxing rings in the dimly lit Brookfield's Gym. He turned left and right, glancing over his shoulders to see Kirsten and Jack in the same position as the three chairs all backed into one another. They formed a triangle with their chairs, all facing out towards the ropes.

"Kirsten! Are you ok?" Tommy asked frantically.

"Yes, I'm fine Tommy, are you?" Kirsten snivelled.

"I can't move," Tommy said as he struggled, clenching his teeth attempting to burst the tie wraps by brute strength alone.

“Ah, how sweet,” Carruthers voice came from the shadows with a sinister delight, “young love checking in on each other before their doom, kind of poetic, don’t you think?”

He moved into what little light there was and crouched by Tommy, close enough that he could smell his pungent after shave. He pulled out a handkerchief from his blazer pocket and wiped the blood which trickled down Tommy’s neck from the blow to the rear of his head. There was perverse intimacy in his actions; he looked like he was taking pleasure from this.

“Fuck you Carruthers, you piece of shit!” Tommy screamed attempting to break out of his shackles and attack his nemesis. He wobbled the chair but made no real progress in escaping.

Carruthers cackled hard in mockery, which prompted his goons to follow suit, the one with the goatee beard was missing though.

“There’s something about a place like this which calls out to me; the blood, the sweat, the tears. The battleground, a place where only the strong survive,” he paced around the ring, circling his three captives, inhaling as though he was sucking the life out of the world, “I have built my empire up over 30 years to the point where I am untouchable and if you think that you are going to come even close to bringing me down when I am so near to walking away, then you’ve got another thing coming. Your dad tried all those years ago, god bless his soul, but he failed…”

“Don’t you dare speak about my father!” Tommy yelled.

"I tried to warn him, I really did. And I meant what I said; he was a good man who tried to help the young people of this town."

"They wouldn't have needed help if it wasn't for you, you twisted freak!" snapped Kirsten.

"Don't judge what you don't understand. I couldn't have your dad poking his nose in business that was... beyond his remit, shall we say? To his credit, he's one of the only men in this town that I haven't been able to intimidate or pay off. It was with a heavy heart that I put a bullet through his skull; an honourable death for an honourable man."

Tommy was furious, "You son of a –"

"Hey! Watch your mouth, I'm getting cranky!" Carruthers growled, "You won't like me when I'm cranky, trust me. Now look, I don't expect you to understand, of course you're going to be mad – it's your dad! I did what I had to do, to protect my interests and maintain my double life. It really has been the perfect crime," he continued, seemingly impressed by his perceived successes, "the face of Granville-upon-sea, the saviour, whose alter ego is the very person that the town needs saving from!" Carruthers sniggered, "Tomorrow I will bow out as the town's most successful and longest serving councillor at my 60th birthday come retirement bash, there will be people queueing up to have their picture taken with me, donations being made, it will be wonderful and nothing you can do can stop it happening because my friends, you won't see the light of day again."

"Go on then," Kirsten interrupted, "What's stopping you?"

"Oh she is a feisty one isn't she?" Carruthers said, impressed by Kirsten's tigress nature, "Well, you silly little bitch, I need to find out who you two mischievous blights have been getting your information from so I can make sure that they're pushing up the daisies alongside you... So, I'm going to have a little fun with you first and if you don't tell me, maybe I'll have to pay your families a visit... How is your little sister by the way, Kirsten?" This threat sent chills down Tommy's spine, not just because it meant his mum and Brother were now in danger, but because he knew that his quest for the truth had also put Kirsten's family at risk. "And you Thomas... How is your mother?" Carruthers smiled a wicked smile, "Ah, your mother, young Theresa, she was a beauty you know?"

"Why are you so interested in my mum? You leave her out of this!" Tommy shouted.

"There's just something about your first that you never forget," Carruthers spoke reminiscently, "I'll never forget the look in her eyes the moment she realised I had completely and utterly taken her for a ride – figuratively and literally. She was a stunner, aged 14 or 15, as soon as I laid eyes on her I had to have her. She was a tough nut to crack though but at that age, they all crack eventually; every single one of them. Once you lure them in with false promises and access to a few adult pleasures, they soon get suckered in; their problem was that they mistook my desires for love and affection... pathetic really." It began to dawn on Tommy where Carruthers was going with this and it knocked him sick to his stomach. *My mum was Carruthers' first victim.*

"You're pathetic! You're a horrible, horrible man!" Kirsten screamed in disgust.

Jack finally mustered the bravery to speak, "I didn't know any of this Tommy, I swear to you I didn't!" The old man sobbed, recognising how much this would be killing his young friend.

The whole room began to spin, Tommy strained and strained but he couldn't break the tie wraps. He felt tears begin to stream down his face, he could feel himself turn pink with rage as snot dribbled from his nose. This is exactly where Carruthers wanted him. The same way he had his victims. He had full control over the situation and watched on as they crumbled in front of him; ultimate cruelty, ultimate power.

"My mum..." Tommy said in disbelief, his whole world came crashing down in front of him. The pain penetrated his mind and body, ploughing its way deep into his very core. Every single piece of his jumbled up existence was beginning to make sense – however absurd – all engineered by Carruthers, the puppet master of Granville. He could see now why his mum was swayed by the path of drugs and self-destruction.

"Don't give him the satisfaction, Tommy!" Kirsten rallied, attempting a valiant defiance, pulling and pushing at her tie wraps but doing more damage to her own skin than anything else.

"You shut your mouth, young lady!" Carruthers commanded, his mood flipping to serious and scary. It was clear why he was so imposing and feared, "Where was I? Oh that's right, your mum yes... I owe her a great deal, she's the catalyst that started all this for me..."

Tommy pulled himself together. He sniffed the snot away as best he could and shook his head to clear the remaining tears. He didn't want to let Carruthers see him this way.

"What kind of man gets off on abusing kids, killing innocent people and ruining lives?" Tommy said, attempting to goad Carruthers. He was aware it was a risky tactic, but he felt like he had nothing to lose.

"Me. That's who. Don't you see, the sex and the drugs are just a bit of fun Thomas, its power that gets me off and boy do I just love it. There's something intoxicating about having total and utter control over somebody, the fear in their eyes, knowing at any moment you can make them do whatever you want them to do and there's nothing anybody can do to stop you..."

"You sick bastard!" Kirsten screamed.

"Quiet! I won't tell you again!" Carruthers commanded, pointing sternly at Kirsten before he continued. "The money isn't bad either. There's only so much money to be made from being a straight laced councillor, you know?" Carruthers said; his brow now coated in sweat, a smear of twisted delight across his face. Tommy found it bizarre how Carruthers was switching between hell-fire crazy one second, to attempting to have, what he clearly believed to be, a rational conversation with them the next.

"So, what, you're just going to give all that up tomorrow after your fancy party?" Tommy quizzed.

Carruthers laughed, "Not a chance. Tomorrow I am bowing out of the public eye, once I've done that,

I can disappear underground into oblivion and enjoy the rest of my days doing what the fuck I want!" his voice rose as he reached the end of his speech, lauding himself and looking as though he may climax.

Carruthers took off his tweed blazer and passed it to the large man in the leather jacket. He rolled up his sleeves and walked around the three chairs one more time.

"Ok people, let's make this easy..."

As he spoke he took a gun from another of his goons, the one whose jaw was slightly ajar following his struggle with Tommy. The gun was an old .44 calibre pistol. He opened the chamber and loaded 6 bullets, before snapping it back shut.

Carruthers began his interrogation, "Where's the girl?"

"What girl?" Tommy said, trying hard to appear confused.

"Wrong answer," Carruthers slammed, before thumping the pistol into the side of Kirsten's head. She screamed in pain, "The girl you went to see who told you about me, I know all about your little trip out of town... Now tell me, where can I find her?" his eyes were protruding now as he pointed the pistol towards Kirsten, wildness dancing inside of him, inciting Tommy to spill the information. It was clear Carruthers lived for these moments.

"Leave them alone!" Jack yelled feebly. It carried no weight though; his shame restricted his voice from reaching the commanding heights it needed to.

At that moment, the thug with the goatee and shaved head, who was keeping watch outside, entered the gym and called out, "Boss! We've got a situation down at the headquarters; we need to go, now!"

"Arghhh!" Carruthers roared in frustration, his hands wide as he looked up to the ceiling, "Remind me what it is I pay you no good pieces of lard for? Do I really need to pack up and leave? What is it, what's the problem?"

The man with the goatee beard answered apprehensively, "It's a code green, Sir."

"Right, well if we have to go, we have to go," Carruthers conceded, "I guess I'll have to wait to deal with you three. Don't worry though; the suspense will make it all the more enjoyable!" He smiled as he put back on his tweed jacket and stepped through the ropes, "You stay here and guard the place," he said to the man with the goatee, "anybody comes anywhere near here, you take care of them, nobody gets in and nobody gets out. As soon as I'm done with the code green, I'll be back to clear this mess up."

And just like that Carruthers and two of his goons were gone. Tommy, Kirsten and Jack were left tied up, in the dimly lit gym, in silence, guarded by one of the heavies of the Smiler organisation, under instruction not to let anybody in, or out.

CHAPTER FOURTEEN

"How could you do this to me, Jack?" Tommy said in despair, all the while wondering how on earth they were going to get out of this predicament. "You were one of the only people in my life I thought I could trust... You're the closet thing I've ever had to a Father!"

"I know what it looks like Tommy, I do and I am so sorry for bringing you here, but you have to believe me, I had no choice and I had no idea this was going to happen – look at me, I'm tied up just like you! Please if I could just explain what happened and then I can only pray that you understand..." Jack pleaded, almost blindly as the three captives all faced away from one another in the dark gym.

"Well it better be good, because if it's not, well, then, well there's pretty much nothing I can do about it right now is there!" Tommy said, greeted with an ironic chuckle from Kirsten, the kind of nervous laugh that made her blush. He was partly annoyed that he had to concede and hear Jack out but was also clinging to some hope that there was an explanation for the perceived betrayal.

"I had no idea he was Smiler before today, I swear to you. He arrived with those blokes earlier on and stuck it right on me; he cleared the gym and got right in my face. You know me, I'm not one for being intimidated son, but this was different, it was like Dr Jekyll and Mr. Hyde, he showed a completely different side to his usual persona – he's normally so jolly, guess it's clear why they call him Smiler, huh? Plus it was four on one and I'm not as spritely as I used to be."

Tommy waited, hoping that Jack had a more solid reason to bring him here than the threat of being beaten up, as awful as that was.

Jack continued, "Anyway, he told me to ask you to come here because he wanted to know what you knew about your dad. I knew something wasn't right; it stunk, so I refused. Then he starts with the threats, says he'll close my gym down. My gym is the only thing keeping this ticker of mine going Tom, you know that. He also says he'll spread rumours that would stick like shit to a blanket, about me and the kids at the gym, awful stuff, the kind of stuff he's into. When he sees I'm still not convinced, he says if I don't get you here without suspicion right now, he'll take the pair of us down to the pier and put a bullet through us... just like he did your old man."

Tommy listened as his friend, fifty years his senior, frantically tried to explain himself. Tears were on the periphery of returning but he managed swallow his sadness. He felt a mixture of emotions, but one thing he didn't feel anymore was betrayal.

He could see clearly that Carruthers had given Jack no choice.

"It knocked me sick Tommy, I didn't know what to do, but he promised me he wouldn't lay a finger on you," Jack sighed shaking his head. "Fat lot of a good a promise is from a despicable bastard like that. I feel foolish and I am sorry for putting you both in this position."

It was heartfelt and Tommy knew it. He took a few breaths and tried to compose himself; he felt completely discombobulated.

"Ok Jack, I understand, he would have got to me sooner or later anyway." Tommy said, relieved to have just one less thing screwing with his head.

"Jack, if I could move right now, I'd give you a hug... but I'm a little tied up," said Kirsten, shattering the ice with her well-timed humour as usual, in an attempt to lift their spirits, "I don't know if you know this but I'm kind of inappropriate with my hugs and hand them out when I'm nervous or excited."

The three of them let out a light chuckle but the severity of their current situation didn't allow for the fear to lift. They were scared, pure and simple.

"What are we going to do?" Tommy asked.

He detected vulnerability in his own voice now. He'd been able to remain so brave and assured throughout this pursuit of the truth surrounding his dad, spurred on by the promise of answers but blissfully unaware, for the most part, of just how earth shattering those answers would be.

He now feared the worst as he was running out of ideas and unfortunately for him, Kirsten and Jack weren't forthcoming with any solutions either. It was almost silent, except for the rain hammering against the window. A streetlight offered a little glow, but it created more shadows than actual light.

In a place where he usually felt so safe and secure, even getting his head punched in, Tommy couldn't have felt more scared and helpless. He mulled over the things he wished he had done and said. He wished he could have helped his mum with her troubles. He wished he would have made more of an effort to spend time with Derek in recent years. He wished he'd realised sooner how he felt about Kirsten and told her.

It's amazing what the fear of death can do to a person's mind. No longer did the heroin habits and the lack of parenting matter, his mum and Derek were his family and he loved them. He just hoped he would get the chance to tell them again, for what would be the first time in as long as he can remember.

With Kirsten, he wasn't sure what his feelings were exactly, *was it love?* That slight doubt still remained as to whether they were just really good friends, a friend who he now found attractive and had enjoyed the slight intimacy they had shared over the last few days and weeks.

Whilst he had to pray for the chance to tell his mum and Derek how he felt again, there was nothing stopping him from letting Kirsten know right now, he may not have much time left with Carruthers due back any minute, on the warpath and thirsty for blood.

"Kirsten, there's something I think I need to tell you. Well, I'm not even sure what it is I need to say,

I'm not very good at this kind of stuff, but I feel like if I don't say something now, I might not get another chance, you know?" Tommy said, rather awkwardly, but given the circumstances he could hardly expect to pull off a Hollywood rom-com performance. Jack smiled.

"What is it, Tommy?" Kirsten said, her voice was pitchy and a little excitable given the circumstances.

It felt as though a cage full of butterflies had just burst open inside his tummy. This was it; the moment of truth where he found out if his friend felt the same, or if he'd completely misread the situation and would remain in solitude with his feelings. He hadn't realised until now, just how much he wanted to tell Kirsten about how his feelings towards her had changed – granted he'd pictured it someplace else with less of the tie wraps, guns, murderers and the probable impending death.

Tommy tried to look round but struggled, he saw in his peripheral vision that Kirsten was looking up and biting her bottom lip in anticipation. He felt a rush of hope and expectation. At this particular moment, maybe facing away from one another wasn't all that bad.

"The thing is," Tommy began, venturing into the unknown, "lately, well, lately I've kind of been, you know –"

Before Tommy could continue, there was a sound of lowered voices that came from outside. All three of their heads jolted to face the door simultaneously. Tommy felt a little embarrassment, he couldn't tell if Kirsten seemed disappointed or relieved at the interruption, but these emotions were immediately replaced by terror. Tommy's heart was pounding out of his chest, the fear of Carruthers returning as well as almost declaring his feelings to Kirsten was taking its toll. It was a deathly thrill.

"Tommy I don't want to die, not like this, not here, not with so much left undone," Kirsten despaired, tears returning to her eyes.

They heard the muffled voices become a little more animated and then loud noise that sounded like the clang of metal. Then silence. The suspense was unbearable. The fact they couldn't see what was going on, that they were so restricted, meant that Tommy's imagination was running away with him and he was positive that Kirsten's and Jack's would be doing the same. *What was happening now? What will happen next?*

The sounds of footsteps were closing in on the entrance to the gym. Tommy, Kirsten and Jack stared firmly at the door as the arrival of their fate was imminent. The door handle slowly began to be drawn down, a crack of light appearing as it opened slowly. The crack of light got wider and a dark figure became visible, stood in the gym doorway. He reached for the light and flicked it on. It was Derek.

"Derek!" Tommy screamed. "Oh my word, are we glad to see you!"

"Tommy, what the heck has gone on here? Come on let's get you out of here..." Derek said as he made his way over towards the ring, his cagoule soaking wet, his hair stuck to his forehead.

"How did you – Where did you –" Tommy couldn't even muster the words to ask the questions he wanted to ask.

The relief washed over his body as their unlikely hero stepped through the ropes and began to clip the tie wraps with his Swiss Army Knife, ironically a 'toy' which Tommy had often teased Derek for carrying with him, simply based on Derek not striking him as the kind of character that would ever need such a tool.

"We've no time to talk mate, we need to get you the hell out of here. I'm guessing you weren't being held in here for a game of tiddlywinks? We can talk once we're safe... Let's go!"

Derek spoke with the kind of assertiveness that surprised Tommy. Derek snapped the final tie wrap which was holding one of Jack's ankles to the chair and they were all but free.

"Who are you? And what have you done with my brother?" Tommy asked sarcastically, impressed and taken aback by Derek's macho bravery and composure in this dreadful situation. "You're right though, we need to move, Carruthers will be back any minute."

"How did you get past the guy on guard?" Kirsten asked, as they scrambled towards the door and their freedom.

The four of them made it to the door. Tommy had grasped Kirsten's hand and they exchanged a glance which said more than any words ever could. They spilled out into the car park to see Carruthers' shaven headed bouncer sprawled out, face down on the concrete.

"I hit him over the head... with that kettle!" Derek said with a serious face, pointing towards a kettle which he'd obviously cast off before entering the gym. Just like that Derek's apparent MI5 agent status was undone by his choice of weapon and he returned to the more familiar identity of Tommy's daft older brother. "What? I found it over there!" Derek said, pointing over to the skip which was a permanent fixture in the Brookfield's gym car park. Tommy smiled inside at his brother justifying his use of kitchenware as a weapon and bringing a whole new meaning to the term 'by any means necessary'.

Just as they thought they were home and free, Jack stalled. He was about 10 yards behind the rest who were almost out of the car park. He looked indecisive, like being able to escape and live wasn't the obvious choice.

"Jack, come on what are you doing? We've got to go, NOW!" Tommy screamed back to his coach and friend.

"Hang on!" Jack shouted as, to the utter disbelief of the others, he turned and ran back into the gym.

"What's he doing? Carruthers will be back any second... He's playing with fire; we've got to go, Tommy!" Kirsten begged.

"I can't leave him, Kirst. Just give him a minute..." said Tommy.

Derek was out of the small concrete car park now and onto the street, his head pivoting both ways, anxious at the anticipated return of his brother's captor, who just so happened to be the Crime Lord of Granville.

"Come on Jack, what you playing at?" Tommy added, this time rhetorical and under his breath as Kirsten tried to pull him towards safety.

It wasn't a busy street at night so any noise of distant traffic triggered a sense of worry and panic. Derek was the first to see them and he froze on the spot; headlights, turning onto Glenwood Street. The car was still in the distance but Derek was close enough to see it was a large 4x4, a Range Rover or Jeep of some description.

"Shit Tommy! Let's go, there's a car coming! It looks like it could be Carruthers!" Derek urged, with a shout disguised as a whisper.

Kirsten looked at Tommy, pain and fear in her eyes, blood on the side of her face from the blow she took from Carruthers. He had to make a decision. Time seemed to slow right down but the rain still poured. Derek was waving his arms and saying something that Tommy couldn't quite grasp. Kirsten was pulling Tommy away from the gym and towards Glenwood Street where they could still make a run for it. The car moved further up the street towards them. Then he appeared. Just in the nick of time Jack came stumbling out the gym carrying some kind of package in his hand. He moved pretty well for a guy in his sixties.

"Jack! Come on let's go!" shouted Tommy, giving in to Kirsten's orders and allowing her to pull him away and begin their move to safety.

They ran out of the car park and onto the street to where Derek was and the four of them stopped in their tracks, like rabbits in the headlights – literally. The car approached, Tommy's heart almost took off up into his mouth. Kirsten gripped Tommy's hand and closed her eyes. Derek's mouth was ajar and Jack was barely just catching his breath. The car drove past. It wasn't Carruthers.

"Ah man! I thought we were done for there!" Derek said, letting out a relieved smile, turning to face the other three. He offered a rather untimely high five but had no takers as they were still frozen on their feet momentarily. Tommy was the first to thaw out.

"What was that all about, Jack?" Tommy ranted.

"No time for that, I'll explain later… quick, let's move!" Jack said, nudging the youngsters in the direction of the dark side of the street, the opposite direction to any traffic, light or life. Tommy understood Jack's plan, he knew they needed to take the road least travelled in order to escape the clutches of Carruthers. They were still deep inside Smiler territory and it would take only a glimpse from one of his crew members and they'd be back tied to those chairs in the blink of an eye. They needed to get off grid and stay there.

They moved as quickly as they could; running where possible, walking and almost crawling in patches, but always moving. They checked both ways down every street, pathway and alley – twice – before they crossed any open space, keeping their backs to the wall and on the lookout for danger. The rain had eased off making visibility a little easier, although that was a bit of a double edged sword in these circumstances; see and more alarmingly *be seen*.

"Woah, man!" Derek said as they skulked in the shadows of the circuit of alleyways that meandered through the back streets off the top of Glenwood

Street. "And I thought you could get high off drugs, but that was a different level, that was some kind of super high; escaping the jaws of a beat down and rescuing you guys." Derek was clearly pleased with himself and whilst Tommy, Kirsten and Jack appreciated what he did and what he was saying, they weren't quite at the stage of revelling yet. Tommy didn't truly believe they were safe yet.

"How did you know where to find us?" Tommy asked, his mind settling down now and attempting to process the remarkable events that had just occurred – his brother, who he'd come to expect absolutely nothing from and who regularly delivered exactly that, had literally just saved them from death and a very painful one at that.

"Well," Derek began; clearly enjoying his new found capabilities, "it took a while for it to sink in what you told me about Smiler and Dad and all that and when I came round I desperately wanted to, erm, well you know, give in to my urges shall we say," Tommy rolled his eyes, Derek was never the most subtle. "But, I realised that you'd said you'd be straight back to finish telling me and you'd been gone ages, then I remembered that Jack had texted you and it was a bit out of the blue, so I came for a walk to check you were alright."

Tommy felt an unfamiliar surge of pride and love rushing through his body. Derek actually came to see if he was ok. Whilst most folk would see this as a given, it was a big deal for Tommy.

Derek continued, "Then when I got towards the gym, I saw it with hardly any lights on and that bald headed fella lurking around outside, so I put two and two together and thought you'd need help. I slipped inside the car park when he wasn't looking and round by the skip, picked myself up whatever I could find, which just so happened to be an old kettle. I got as close as I could and then distracted him by asking him for a lighter and well, you know the rest." Derek looked mighty pleased with himself; the sense of achievement must have been overwhelming for somebody who saw going to the shop and back as a daily conquest.

"Thank you Derek," Tommy said, "I mean that, you've really come through for us there bro." He smiled, seeing a different side to his brother, one he'd not seen in a heck of a long time.

"Yes, I'll second that," Kirsten added.

"Me too," said Jack, "Now, we need somewhere safe to go so we can figure out what the hell we're going to do."

There was a moments silence before Kirsten spoke up, "I know a place."

The four of them continued their journey through the gauntlet of Granville's back streets, attempting to avoid contact with anyone if they could. They hid behind parked cars and in doorways when they needed to. Whilst pacing through the night, they did their best to bring Derek up to date on a few of the details which occurred inside the gym and led to them being tied up, although they couldn't quite catch their breath enough to answer all of Derek's many questions.

Their journey soon had a sanctuary of safety in sight as they turned the corner to see the lights beaming out of the windows. It was 10pm on a Saturday night, where else but the Junction pub.

CHAPTER FIFTEEN

The wall of noise hit them instantly as Kirsten pushed open the doors to the Junction. A mixture of music, laughter, shouting and loud voices provided the familiar Saturday night melody, accompanied by the smell of cigarettes, stale ale and the heat that busy pubs often had. 'Hotter the pub, more they drink.' Kirsten's Uncle Bill would always say.

Kirsten, Tommy, Derek and Jack made their way into the pub, Tommy was still feeling on edge and shaken up after their horrendous ordeal. They were greeted with a few odd looks, probably because they looked damp and sober, but on the whole it was exactly what they needed – a friendly welcome. Barry the doorman was the first to greet them.

"Evening folks" he said, with his usual charming grin. For a big, imposing bloke, he sure had a friendly smile.

The usual crowd of lively lads were packed around the pool table and emptying their change into the jukebox to keep the music flowing as steadily as the lager. You could hear anything from AC/DC to

James Brown in the Junction; its reputation of housing the best jukebox in town was almost as renowned as its reputation for turning a blind eye to under-age drinking.

Uncle Bill saw their arrival and waved them over towards his end of the bar. Whilst he wasn't used to seeing the four of them hanging out as a group at the Junction on a Saturday night all that often, it wasn't beyond the realm of possibility for them to be together, so he mustn't have thought too much of it.

Janine McAllister was busy pulling pints behind the bar and, despite her initial look of uneasiness at the sight of Tommy and Kirsten entering the pub, she managed to offer them a slight smile and nod of acknowledgement. Janine was a machine when it came to work and actually enjoyed the busy periods, so a nod and a slight smile was probably as good as they were going to get for now.

Derek's old friend, Dorian, was in the pub too and a little merry to say the least. Upon seeing Derek, he almost spilled his pint down himself in delight and disbelief. He wiped the lager froth from his top lip, slammed his pint down and threw his arms around Derek, getting to work on catching up and reacquainting. It occurred to Tommy at that moment that this was the sign of true friends; however long it has been since they've spoken or seen one another, it seemed completely natural to pick up right where it left off.

Once Derek was engulfed into Dorian's excitable embrace, Jack followed towards the bar to see Bill about fixing him up with a stiff drink.

"Whiskey please, Bill," Jack said. "Large!"

Bill smiled, probably assuming Jack had just had one of those stressful days, little did he know just how stressful.

Kirsten grabbed Tommy by the hand and pulled him to one side. She looked serious but tried to hide it with a smile. Tommy thought she looked nervous. She held him by both hands as they stood facing each other, matching bruises on each of their wrists from the plastic tie wraps; a mark of trauma, but also a mark of solidarity. Tommy smiled an awkward smile back. He could feel Kirsten's pulse at the pressure point on her wrist, it was fast and strong, her heart must have been beating like the gallop of a couple of prize race horses.

"What's up?" Tommy said; his eyes fixed on Kirsten's and hers on his. Despite her earlier tears, Kirsten's were still as crystal clear as they always were. That new feeling that Tommy had been experiencing lately returned, only now it was stronger; the huge throb in his tummy, his heart bouncing from stomach to throat and back again. He'd never felt so uncomfortably comfortable.

"Tommy listen," Kirsten began. Tommy gently wiped away some of the rain water which sat on her cheek following their walk in the elements. Kirsten closed her eyes savouring Tommy's soft touch, his shaking hand showing he was just as nervous as her. She opened her eyes and continued, "I think I know what you were going to say earlier, well, I hope I do, and even if not I'm going to say this anyway. Tonight's events have taught me that life is too short. When we were tied up, I just wanted you to know that, I feel, well I –"

Kirsten was interrupted by a drunken man tripping and bulldozing into them, breaking them from their trance. If it wasn't for the collision into Tommy and Kirsten, the man would have almost certainly hit the floor.

"Who put that there?" The drunken man said to nobody, slurring his words and trying to steady himself on his feet. Then he turned and revealed who he was.

It was Mr. Hargreaves. Tommy stiffened up. Fear kicked in and as much as he wanted to run, he was rooted to the spot where he stood. He did manage to guide Kirsten to safety behind him. The pub was so busy and loud that nobody noticed the two of them face to face. Young Tommy Dawson and a drunken Mr Hargreaves just looked like any other couple of punters in the pub having a chit chat. It was at this moment Tommy realised he wasn't safe, even here at the Junction.

"You!" Mr. Hargreaves raged, his face frowning as he swayed and pointed towards Tommy, although his aim was a little off. He looked just like his son; horrible and hostile only with more wrinkles and greying hair. Mr Hargreaves' eyes were glazed over and before he could muster the words to continue, Tommy found his voice.

"Look Mr. Hargreaves, I know you've been looking for me, well you're too late. I've already seen Smiler and I know exactly what's happened and all about his schemes. You'll have to kill me before I let this go!" Tommy was pumped up; his near death experience had given him a foolhardy sense of confidence in the face of confrontation.

"Smiler?" Mr. Hargreaves questioned, looking confused, "What on earth are you talking about, boy? I've been looking for you to tell you to back off and leave my son alone! I've heard about you head butting him at school... I know he can be an obnoxious little so and so, but you lay a finger on him again and you'll have me – and the police – to deal with, as well as my lawyers, not that you paupers could ever pay any damages, understand?"

Tommy looked at Kirsten and fought hard to hold back the laughter. All this time he'd believed Mr. Hargreaves to be involved in Smiler's organisation and was afraid he was looking for him. The head butt to Craig Hargreaves seemed so small and insignificant now, let alone it seemed like a million years ago. He also felt a sense of relief though – that's one more person who isn't involved with Smiler when it had started to feel as though the whole town might have been turned.

"I'm sorry Mr. Hargreaves, I understand you looking out for your son," Tommy turned on the charm, sensing Mr. Hargreaves was the kind of guy who would appreciate his ego being massaged a little. "I admire it in fact, I only wish I had a parent who looked out for me the way you're doing for Craig... It won't happen again."

Mr. Hargreaves smiled, appreciating Tommy's respectful response, his drunken state not allowing him to pick up on the slightly facetious tone which Tommy conveyed.

He ruffled Tommy's hair in a patronising manner, consistent with the image he portrayed; a snobby, self-indulgent twit. He stumbled off towards the bar and called out for another drink.

Tommy turned to Kirsten and they burst into laughter at how ridiculous their original theory was and how drunk Mr. Hargreaves was. They also shared a chuckle at how the mighty Craig Hargreaves needed his dad to fight his battles – if only the rest of Wellington High knew as much.

Once they'd laughed a little and recomposed themselves, their eyes met and locked on to that loving gaze once more. Tommy waited for Kirsten to pick up from where she left off prior to the interruption, but he sensed she was waiting for him to take the baton and finished what he had started in Jack's gym. Their stare lingered, but neither wanted to take the plunge for a third time lucky.

Tommy was longing to just lean in and kiss Kirsten's soft lips. They held hands again and he gently caressed Kirsten's hand with his thumb; a small but significant signal of affection. For a moment, it felt as though they were the only two people in the room.

"Do you two want a drink, or are you just going to keep staring at each other all night?" Jack's interruption was brash and untactful, consistent with a man of his age. Tommy snapped back into the room, reluctantly. A little embarrassed, they let go of one another's hands and turned towards the bar to get their order in; pint of Carling and a Bacardi and diet coke.

"What are we going to do?" Tommy said after he'd taken the first sip of his drink. Derek had managed to escape the clutches of Dorian for a few minutes and he joined Tommy, Kirsten and Jack on a table in the only quiet spot in the pub.

"We need help, Tommy," Kirsten responded assertively, "I know you were keen on keeping people out of this to keep them safe, but it's past that now. We need all the help we can get!"

"I'm with her on this one Tom," Jack said, agreeing with Kirsten's stance, "I get that you don't want to go to the police after what happened to your dad, but times have changed –"

"Yeah, my dad has a close friend who is a copper, it might be worth..." Kirsten paused as a couple of people walked past their table towards the toilet. She lowered her voice and they all leaned in to listen, "...it might be worth my dad reaching out to him. If I talk to my dad and explain, he'll protect us, he'll protect us all." Kirsten was almost sounding optimistic.

Derek chirped up, he'd already sunk two and a half beers, bought and paid for by anybody but him of course, "Whatever we do, we have to act quickly. By now Carruthers will have returned to Jack's gym and seen that his prey – aka you three – is no longer tied up waiting for him. He's going to want to iron that situation out real quick."

Tommy sat there feeling nervy and tense; it appeared to be a common theme amongst the group as the mood dropped significantly, minds deep in thought. The prospect of Carruthers bursting through the door any minute with his band of bruisers was terrifying. Then Tommy had a thought.

"No, no he won't." He said, "He's not going to want to risk making a mess that he can't clean up without a fuss, not this close to his retirement bash tomorrow. He made it clear that that's a priority for him... That means we just need to stay out of his way for now."

"We need somewhere quiet to talk about this and with us needing as much help as we can get, what do you say I have a quiet word with Uncle Bill and see how he feels about us staying behind after the pub closes to have a chat?" Kirsten proposed.

Tommy thought about it and nodded in approval, fiddling with his beer mat. He was struggling for ideas and maybe Kirsten was right - *the more help, the better.*

"Telling the police what we know isn't enough, he's greasing too many palms in high powered positions; the accusations would get squashed before we even left the station." Tommy said, determined and steely as he took another sip of his drink. "No, we need a smarter plan, a plan to expose him, so it's beyond doubt for all to see and I think I know just the place we can do it."

The last orders bell came and went and slowly, but surely, the Saturday night crowd began to exit the Junction. Old Teddy Phillips had to be woken up from his usual spot after he fell asleep on his stool propped up against the bar. 'Crunchy' was still chewing somebody's ear off even as they were walking out the door. The lively lads left, chanting a clichéd chorus of the famous Thin Lizzy anthem, as they made their way out of the pub, probably heading towards the town centre to a few of the bars that opened a bit later.

Once the final person was shown the exit by Barry and he too himself said 'Goodnight', Carol shut the door and locked it, pottering off into the back to start cleaning up in the kitchen. Tommy, Kirsten, Jack and Derek were joined at their table by Kirsten's Uncle Bill and a round of drinks. Janine McAllister drifted over to that area but kept her distance and continued to wipe down tables. She was clearly wary but also appeared intrigued by the secret meeting.

"Right, what's all this then?" Bill opened up with a smile, blissfully unaware that the information he was about to receive would not only be huge, but also dangerous.

The pub was in darkness, but for the lights over the bar which lit up the spirit and liquor optics. The room was shadowy from the street light coming through the windows and the mood was tense.

Tommy, Kirsten and Jack proceeded to tell Bill what had happened over the last few weeks, culminating in this evening's terrifying events at Jack's gym. Derek chipped in with details of his heroics, but mostly sat back and absorbed all the information again and took advantage of yet another free drink.

Derek seemed to be enjoying this change of routine, despite appearing a little uncomfortable. He scratched at his skin a little and exhaled heavily a couple of times expressing his distress, but in the main he hid the signs of withdrawal well. Tommy picked up on this and was proud of his brother for sticking with it and not running to hide under a rock – or pipe.

It must have been nice for Derek to have something more important to be involved in to act as a distraction, however dangerous it might have been. Tommy imagined it would have allowed him to focus on something other than his itchy skin and the shooting pains up and down his legs, which he assumed Derek would be starting to feel right about now. Tommy was happy to be doing something with his brother, he was under no illusion that his body would have needed a fix by now but took comfort in the fact that Derek's mind was so enthralled by the goings on that he was determined to keep his cravings at bay and was managing to do a good job of it, for the moment. He had to get up and pace around at intervals and was beginning to sweat a little, but reminders of his heroics and a few pats on the back were helping to keep him afloat. It wasn't all fairy tales though; Tommy noticed Derek had to slip a couple of diazepam down with his pint of lager, which would help to take the edge off.

"That councillor fella? Are you sure?" Bill quizzed having heard the full story, struggling to link the squeaky clean councillor image with the ruthless, vindictive reputation of Smiler.

"100%. And Bill, I know what you're thinking, 'oh, it's only Jim Carruthers'," Jack said, sensing Bill might be considering retribution for his niece, as was Bill's way, "but its legit – the real deal; guns, death threats, murder, everything you've ever heard about Smiler... it's him. I was as scared, if not more scared, than these two, they were brave as lions." Jack said, nodding towards Kirsten and Tommy, who smiled modestly.

Suddenly, there was a noise by the toilets, just out of sight. Someone was there.

"Who's that? Come out now!" Bill commanded. There was movement from behind the mahogany wood panelling, which separated the main area of the pub with the toilets. A shady figure could be seen through the stained glass.

With his hands in the air and a slightly apologetic look, it was Dorian who staggered out into the open. He walked over to the table and gave a sheepish smile and a nod.

"I'm sorry, Bill. I was in the toilet and when I came out and heard you lot talking, I thought I best not interrupt. I was going to wait, but then I lost my footing and banged into the wall." Dorian said, with a hiccup or two, "So what's this I hear about guns and death threats?"

Dorian pulled up a stool and casually joined the group. He helped himself to some peanuts from the table as he revealed he'd overheard way too much. By this point Janine McAllister had put her cloth down and was all ears. Tommy looked at Kirsten and her at Bill; they all looked back towards Jack in dismay, before Tommy eventually spoke.

"Well, seeing as you've heard too much as it is, you may as well join us – but this is top secret Dorian, it's huge, once you're in, you're in and to be honest, the odds aren't looking too good, mate." Tommy said, feeling a little uneasy about his role as leader, especially with his brother's oldest friend and the old guard of Bill and Jack.

"Hey listen, I'm loyal to the core and if my pals need help, I'm here for them... init Derek!" Dorian said as he slapped Derek on the back. Dorian seemed to be buzzed and brought a bit of comradery to proceedings; Tommy only hoped he was still as enthused when he understood the full picture.

The group set to work on trying to figure out a way they could not only get out of this situation alive, but also bring down Carruthers once and for all. Of course, Bill and Dorian had plenty of questions but the rest brought them up to speed.

By this point, Janine had moved from a spectator perched on a bar stool, to a participant around the table, contributing where she could. She shared with the group that this felt as though she finally had an opportunity, however slight, to get a sense of justice for her old school friend.

The gang were buoyed by each other's bravery, loyalty and passion for justice and worked into the early hours on trying to think of a plan that could have the desired effect, bar snacks and refreshments on tap, supplied by Bill and Janine.

Although Tommy was fully focused on the mission to destroy Carruthers, a space in his head was reserved for his mum. He was disturbed by the revelation tonight and just how much Carruthers got off by telling him. He was starting to think about his mum in a different way. His attention switched from the drugs, alcohol, unemployment and bitterness, which he had believed to define his mum, to this heinous act that denied her of a fulfilling life. Rather than the self-made victim he'd always assumed she was, he now saw that the mental, physical and emotional torture she endured as a girl was nothing short of a life sentence, before she'd even left school.

No wonder she was cold, self-destructive and short of positive ways to cope. How could I have been so wrong?

Despite the enormity of the task at hand and the fact that they almost died that very evening, Tommy felt comfortable in his surroundings and he could see that Kirsten did too. They were with people they could rely on, despite Carruthers' efforts to dismantle that level of trust. Deep down however, they all knew this was a monumental task. They were in way over their heads, playing heroes in a game which has no reset button.

The all mighty Smiler, an urban legend who had tormented the streets of Granville for 30 years, his alter ego – Jim Carruthers – an extremely well-connected man who had been getting away with abuse and murder for decades without so much as a rumour, never mind any media attention or meaningful police involvement.

How on earth was this band of misfits going to expose him for what he was? They brought a completely new meaning to the term 'underdogs'. This was their Everest and they barely had a pair of hiking boots between them.

CHAPTER SIXTEEN

It was Sunday the 14th November, 8:43pm. Cllr Jim Carruthers was chatting to guests and posing for photographs at his 60th Birthday/Retirement bash. He was still seething that his captors had escaped his clutches the night before. He knew that it was a mess that needed cleaning up, but not tonight. Tonight was all about him and he was set on soaking up all the accolades that were coming his way. Nobody was going to ruin that for him.

The dinner was being held at the Whitmore Hotel, one of the more well thought of places on the seafront of Granville. It was a slightly aged hotel now, but its grand function room, the King Louis suite, with patterned red carpets that were once plush and sparkling chandeliers, still made it the go-to place for those wanting to throw a fancy event. It was perfect for a grand occasion such as this one.

The who's-who of Granville-upon-sea were here tonight to celebrate the wonderful career of their devoted councillor, none of them suspecting that what he really stood for was power, greed and control. *Fools!*

The room was filled with ball gowns and tuxedos, champagne flutes and table service, high-end décor and fancy flower displays. As he'd requested, there was a string quartet performing gracefully on stage and bringing an air of elegance to the proceedings, to the side of them stood a lectern with a microphone – for the speeches of course.

He stood proud wearing his Dolce and Gabbana two-piece suit, jet black with a matching dickie bow tie. His top button felt tight and he was warm. He pulled at the collar of his shirt in an attempt to free some of the air trapped inside. It must have been the room and all of the extra-special attention. He didn't often feel flustered but this was getting close.

Tonight was the night that he received the well-deserved plaudits for his long and illustrious career. All the hours both in the public eye of this town – and dirtying his hands in the rotten underground – would all come to fruition tonight. He just needed to smile and get through the evening, clear up the mess which that little swine, Tommy Dawson, had created and then disappear into the wind towards a relaxing retirement filled with his deepest desires. *Piece of cake.*

***

There were a couple of security guards roaming the floor and some outside at the entrance to the suite taking tickets and checking bags. These guys had the appearance of a legitimate security outfit, with earpieces and smart suits. They were a private firm, above board and well paid for. They weren't the scum who did Smiler's dirty work in the shadows at night, no neck tattoos or guns in holsters. In public, Carruthers had to maintain his clean and orderly image. That's exactly why Tommy, Kirsten and the rest of the gang thought this to be the place that they had their best shot at getting to him.

There was a tap on the fire exit door at 8:45pm, as agreed. Serena Rimmer, waitress at the Whitmore and previous romantic acquaintance of Dorian who now kept in touch as friends, made her way down the corridor and opened it. Waiting there were Tommy, Kirsten, Jack and Dorian.

"Hurry up!" Serena said, waving the four of them in. "I swear to god Dorian, if I get in any trouble for this –"

"You won't, I promise," Dorian said; cool as a cucumber, "have you got the wristbands?" he asked.

Serena passed them four of the wristbands, which the party goers received once handing in their tickets. It was a system that allowed people to come and go to the toilets, cigarette breaks and such like without just letting any old random person in off the street – theoretically. Serena held her hand out. Dorian obliged and handed her the agreed £20.

"And Steady Eddie; is he good to go?" Dorian enquired.

Eddie was another of his friends who worked at the hotel too. Dorian had saved him from a load of trouble a while ago, so Eddie was in his debt. Dorian felt it was the perfect time to call in that favour.

"So he says yes, but you know what Eddie is like! I'm not even going to ask what this is all about; nobody can be that desperate to get into this 60th party with a load of coffin dodgers, surely?"

Serena closed the fire exit and shuffled off down the corridor not waiting for, nor expecting, an answer from Dorian.

The four of them stood at the end of the corridor of the Whitmore hotel, toilets to their left, function room straight ahead. Tommy felt pumped up and adrenalized, he was highly stressed but it all felt a little surreal. They'd come this far now, there was no going back.

"Let's go over the plan one more time..." Tommy began, before clarifying their intentions.

Jack and Dorian had scrubbed up pretty well with a view to blending in the best they could. Jack had a light grey three-piece suit on and wore a flat cap and some thick rimmed glasses to help disguise his face, not that anybody would have thought them crazy enough to have come here tonight. Dorian went for the classic penguin suit and, with his hair combed over and beard trimmed, he looked rather dashing.

Tommy felt uncomfortable having thrown together an outfit. He wore a mixture of borrowed clothes; Jack's old navy blue suit, Dorian's white shirt and red tie and his own trusty school shoes. It left him feeling, yet again, like the poor kid who relied on hand-me-downs, but now wasn't the time for self-pity. He was used to feeling this way and had made his circumstances part of his armoury. Kirsten didn't seem to mind and that was good enough for him. Especially given the way she looked tonight.

Kirsten was dazzling, a radiating beauty. She wore a long, black dress to the floor. She could have passed for twice her age; her make up classy and subtle, her hair tied up exposing her beauty. She'd also managed to conceal the cut and surrounding bruise she had at the side of her head, just above her temple, courtesy of Carruthers and his nasty blow the previous evening.

Kirsten had mention to Tommy on the way here that she'd actually enjoyed getting glammed up, it distracted her from the near suicide mission they were intending to embark upon. Tommy just wished that they were heading to a real party where they could laugh and dance and if the opportunity presented itself, he could finally find an excuse to kiss her. Instead, he had to focus on the task at hand, remain unseen and stick to the plan.

They put on their wristbands and split up in an attempt to remain a little more inconspicuous. Jack and Dorian went on ahead and Kirsten and Tommy waited a little before making their way, hand in hand, towards the entrance of the King Louis suite. Tommy and Kirsten watched on as Dorian began to get into character, laughing, joking and pretending to be merry – his theory being that at a party, it's the loud ones who look like they belong there.

Whatever he did, it worked, as he and Jack slipped past security with a flash of their wristbands and not an iota of difficulty. They were in. Now it was Tommy and Kirsten's turn. They'd hung back a little bit from Dorian and Jack so there was still about 15 yards until they reached the entrance, but it was dead straight ahead; nowhere to hide as they approached.

There were three security guards on the door, all staring straight ahead at the two teenagers approaching. They were transfixed and Tommy felt as though they'd been sussed out. He began to feel the drops of sweat trickle down his back; his heart raced so much he could feel his pulse in his ear, a rhythmic bass drum that was almost muting the surrounding party atmosphere.

Tommy felt as though he was walking through quick sand, his legs had turned to jelly and he desperately wanted to turn back. Kirsten squeezed Tommy's hand as they reached the doorman. She looked calm on the surface but Tommy could feel her hands become clammy.

Surprisingly, or not so surprisingly at all, they didn't pay Tommy much attention, with all three doormen taking a not-so-subtle interest in Kirsten. Their eyes were all over her and they made no effort to hide it. Tommy may as well have been invisible.

"Good evening madam... Sir, please can we see tickets or wristbands?" The first doorman said, politely with a shady smile and an undertone of sleaze. Kirsten flashed her wristband and smiled, walking ahead to allow Tommy to show his. Once the doorman had craned his neck back around to face Tommy, he had a quick look at his wristband and let him through before turning his attention back to Kirsten to gawp at her walking off into the room.

They were almost past security, with one foot in the King Louis suite, when the second doorman spoke, "Excuse me," Tommy froze, struck by a bolt of fear, he felt for sure they were busted, "can I just check your bag, please? Its protocol I'm afraid."

Kirsten looked up and smiled trying to keep her composure, "Sure, no problem at all."

She sashayed back over towards the doormen, believing it better to keep them focussing on her. Better that than them realise they were actually a couple of imposters. Tommy couldn't believe it but he was actually a little jealous, although it made him chuckle inside at how Kirsten was playing these slathering cavemen. Kirsten had her bag checked and they were in. They scurried to find a dark corner to blend in with the crowd and wait for their moment.

They had to make a couple of sharp turns before they found a space that they were comfortable with. One was to avoid Carruthers' assistant who was pottering around and mingling with guests. The other was a quick dash away from their Headteacher from school, Mr Turner, who seemed to be enjoying himself with Mrs Turner, helping himself to the passing champagne and hors d'oeuvres.

Once settled, Tommy exchanged a nod with Jack and Dorian and lifted two champagne flutes from a passing waiter's tray; he took a sip from one and passed the other to Kirsten. Her hand trembled slightly as she took it, clumsily spilling some in the process. She took a sip, glanced around and casually patted down the spillage on her dress, hand and arm with a napkin.

Finally, they settled and were able to fix their eyes on Carruthers. He was near the front by the stage, posing for photographs with his guests. With every flash of the camera, his wicked smirk highlighted exactly why he had adopted the name Smiler.

It was eating Tommy up inside. He stood staring at the man that had destroyed everything in his life; his father's murderer, his mother's abuser, like an evil puppet master dictating his whole existence. He so desperately wanted to run over to him and shout out everything he'd found out. If he did though, he risked blowing it all. He'd be frogmarched out – the crazy ramblings of an underprivileged kid, Father left him and Mother is a drug addict. Carruthers would probably turn it into some kind of political publicity stunt. No, that wasn't the way to do it, not yet. They kept their heads down and waited it out.

At 9:30pm, there was the chiming noise of somebody tapping a glass with their knife to indicate an imminent speech. Kirsten and Tommy looked up and the Master of Ceremonies was up on stage, looking extremely smart, a dinner jacket with tails and a maroon, dickie bow tie.

"Ladies and Gentlemen," he announced, "I'd like to introduce to you your host for the evening; a man who has served this town so honourably over the last 30 years. His hard work and dedication towards making Granville a better place has been second to none..."

"Look at him," Tommy whispered to Kirsten, seething, "and these lot, lapping it up like he's some kind of saviour... I hate him!"

Kirsten placed her hand in Tommy's gently. He felt her touch and his shoulders, which had tensed up and almost touched his ears, relaxed a little.

The Master of Ceremonies was reaching the end of his speech, "… So, ladies and gentlemen, without further ado, please raise the roof, for Councillor Jim Carruthers!"

The room burst into a sickening applause. There was cheering, whistling and lots of clapping, except for four people. Amongst the crowd stood four very defiant people who refused to applaud based on what they knew about the *real* Jim Carruthers. Jack and Dorian glanced over at Tommy and Kirsten and gave them a nod of support. Carruthers made his way up towards the lectern, waving and smiling, his humility as false as every single policy he'd ever stood for.

The crowd settled and Carruthers cleared his throat.

"Thank you, thank you, you are too kind. Firstly I'd like to start by sharing my gratitude and humbleness, as the privilege has been mine to serve you all these years. I want to say a huge thank you to each and every one of Granville's community, without your support I would not have been able to do half the things I have over my career…"

"Give me a break, without the community his drug empire wouldn't have taken off he means…" Tommy whispered to Kirsten, before a lady wearing a red chiffon scarf took exception to the sound of his chattering. She whipped her head round, scowled and shushed him.

"We have not had it all our own way; it has been a tough rollercoaster with lots of lows but fortunately plenty of highs too. We have accomplished many things together; winning best seaside resort 5 years running in the 90's – an accolade I am sure we will return to collect in the near future, when our schools attain an Ofsted score of good or outstanding – only the best schools will do for our children, when we received recognition for the most voluntary hours committed by one community in the year 2000, as part of the national Millennium volunteering drive, hosting the 1994 and 2002 National Youth Games – an honour to be trusted to host such a prestigious event for young people from every corner of the UK, cleaning up our parks, going green and improving our recycling capabilities as a community by 400%, opening the country's first Women's refuge centre, a huge step forward in eradicating the heinous domestic violence and abuse which goes on up and down the UK..."

"He's got a bloody nerve!" Kirsten scorned under her breathe to Tommy, making sure nobody around them heard. Not like they would have, they were too busy gazing at the stage, sucked in by Carruthers' lies and deceit. Even the lady with the red chiffon scarf was too engrossed.

Carruthers continued, "... and many, many more positive stories and highlights along the way. I must say I am looking forward to retirement, some time to myself to find a new hobby perhaps, although I will be sad to leave my responsibilities behind. But, departing my role will be much easier looking back on all of my achievements with a smile. My biggest achievement however... is you. You are the reason I have kept going. Chatting to you in the street, in community centres, at local forums, polling booths, door to door, watching you grow from children to parents, to grandparents in some cases... woops! I'm showing my age, although I think the balloons in the room give that away!"

The room erupted with laughter. Tommy felt like vomiting.

"It is you, the people of Granville that I salute this very evening. Thank you!"

The audience applauded once again, stronger than the previous rounds of clapping, the noise was almost deafening and it kept growing. Jim Carruthers waved to the crowd and bowed as though he was the star of a Broadway musical, taking centre stage, epitomising his sociopathic tendencies.

Jack and Dorian had shuffled their way over to Tommy and Kirsten by this point. The four of them stared at the stage, a gaping hole of defiance in the middle of a gullible, tipsy and jubilant horde.

The noise settled a little, the clapping ceased and the Master of Ceremonies made his way on to the stage to conclude the speeches and no doubt trigger another round of applause for their supposed loyal councillor, who stood, smug faced with sweat glistening in the spotlight that beamed down on him. It was the kind of spotlight that made it difficult to see beyond the light when it shines your way and must have been the reason Carruthers was still yet to spot Tommy and his troops in the dark crowd.

The Master of Ceremonies looked and held his hand out towards Carruthers, but before he could open his mouth, the screen behind them flickered on and the lights dimmed.

An excitable '*Wooo!*' rose from the anticipative audience. Carruthers and the MC looked at one another, slightly perplexed.

"What's this?" Carruthers said, with a modest smirk, "You've not gone and made a video in my honour, have you? You'll get me all embarrassed!"

The crowd laughed. But the MC didn't look convinced. Carruthers seemed to pick up on this and it looked to unsettle him a little.

"Erm, I'm sorry ladies and gentlemen, we must have a technical hitch," said the MC feebly.

Then the video appeared. It was a little fuzzy and the colour wasn't great. It looked like CCTV footage, either that or a homemade video of some description.

"What's this then?" Carruthers asked through a forced smile, before lowering his voice so only the MC could hear, "I don't know what's going on here but I suggest you get this shit sorted out, quick, or I'll have you at the back of that dole queue before the morning!"

The MC looked over unnerved towards the tech guy behind the controls for some answers. The tech guy and all round general dogsbody at the hotel was Eddie Parsons, or Steady Eddie as he was known by his friends. By this point, Dorian had made his way over towards the enclosure which housed the digital, lighting and sound equipment and stood by as his friend, Eddie, played dumb to what was going on, flicking switches and pressing buttons as though that was going to fix the perceived error.

The video played on and it became a little clearer what it was. It was a video taken by what looked like a hidden camera set up in a boxing gym. The light was tricky, but with the right editing, it had been made much brighter. There were three people tied up in a boxing ring and a man circling them inside. Then came the undeniable and unmistakable sound of the man's voice.

"I couldn't have your dad poking his nose in business that was... beyond his remit, shall we say? To his credit, he's one of the only men in this town that I haven't been able to intimidate or pay off. It was with a heavy heart that I put a bullet through his skull; an honourable death for an honourable man."

The audience gasped in horror as they watch the man they had just been swooning over admit to such terrible acts. The man they had entrusted with the safety and progression of their community for so long.

"What is this rubbish?" Carruthers roared, "What's all this nonsense, turn it off, NOW!" he yelled, his face scarlet with rage. He scanned the audience, not knowing whether to try and play it down, laugh it off or run. Then he saw him. Tommy Dawson.

"It's over Carruthers," Tommy said boldly as he stepped forward, "Or should I say, Smiler?"

Yet again there were gasps of disbelief and dismay in the crowd. The video continued to play out the scene from Jack's boxing gym the previous night; the confessions, the threats and the striking of Kirsten with his gun. The whispers flew around the darkened room, like the noise crickets make – you can't see them, but you can hear them.

"You!" Carruthers said, his fat index finger pointing with rage towards Tommy, who stood with Kirsten on one shoulder and Jack on another, "You little swine! Get him out! Get rid of that little tramp!" he barked, his orders falling on deaf ears as nobody responded.

Carruthers looked up to find the whole audience staring at him; some frowning, some in total shock. The room resembled an old fashioned Tuppenny Nudger, as pennies began to drop everywhere.

"I'll never forget the look in her eyes the moment she realised I had completely and utterly taken her for a ride – figuratively and literally. She was a stunner, aged 14 or 15, as soon as I laid eyes on her I had to have her. She was a tough nut to crack though but at that age, they all crack eventually; every single one of them. Once you lure them in with false promises and access to a few free highs, they soon get suckered in; their problem was that they mistook my desires for love and affection... pathetic really."

Tommy spoke again, louder this time, addressing the whole room, "All these years this man has been conning you, deceiving you, failing you. He is a liar, he has polluted the streets with drugs and crime and bent the system that was supposed to protect us, so far out of shape that we no longer feel safe or cared for. This man right here is Smiler; an abusive bastard and he murdered my father, Timothy Dawson! "

"It's all lies!" Carruthers screamed, sweat pouring, but it was no good. The video wasn't lying, it was condemning.

Tommy turned to face Carruthers, "I guess you didn't expect my friend Jack here to set up his camera and catch your little confession party, did you?"

He was beginning to enjoy this, watching on as Carruthers squirmed behind the lectern, his eyes frantically looking towards anyone for support. Tommy couldn't leave it there, now he had Carruthers on the ropes, he craved to rub salt so deeply into the wounds that he would begin to know what it feels like to be helpless, the way he'd made so many others feel.

Tommy continued, "You must be kicking yourself Jim, all these years of being so careful, undone by a 16 year old and his mates. You see, when you came round to Jack's gym throwing threats around and demanding he tricked me into coming there or you'll have his gym shut down, he sensed he needed some insurance, didn't you Jack?" Jack nodded with a big smile, taking off his thick rimmed glasses, his disguise no longer needed as they were almost home and dry. "So when he went into his office to grab his phone, he set his camera up hoping it might catch something that was said or done – what are the chances he'd catch it all on video!" Tommy laughed with irony, "It's all on there..." he continued, "You admitting to murder, extortion, to abusing children – EVERYTHING!" He paused, "And that is what you call... Check... mate."

The sound of low jeering began to herald from the crowd as they turned on their deceitful and poisonous councillor. The security guards, who hadn't expected much to do at all this evening other than checking out the wristbands and the ladies, began to move a little closer to the stage as they must have sensed a mutiny arising.

Carruthers was trapped and he looked like knew it. His eyes darted between the crowd and the exits, desperate for an escape or helping hand. The security guards edged onto the stage towards the left hand side, Carruthers began to move to the right, away from the lectern with which he'd propped himself up by these last couple of minutes.

As the guards approached, Carruthers suddenly put his hand into his jacket and pulled out his .44 calibre pistol, pointing it towards Tommy. The room panicked into a frenzy as people tried to scarper to safety. There was mass fear as the crowd darted in every direction, like insects caught in a thunderstorm. There were piercing screams and the sound of deafening shouting, except for Tommy, everything seemed to slow right down.

He found himself staring at Carruthers, straight into the abyss of his evil eyes; a momentary stare down, hero against villain. Then Carruthers squeezed the trigger.

BANG!

CHAPTER SEVENTEEN

The security guard closest to Carruthers pounced on him immediately, belligerently pinning him to the floor. A second security guard made his way over a split second later and stamped his size 11 boot on top of Carruthers' hand, which held the gun. He plucked it from his grasp and passed it to the third security guard who took it to safety, before turning his attention back to Carruthers, who was wriggling and raging like a man possessed.

The first two guards had to think fast, as the Police would still be a while off. Granville Police Commissioner Brian Phillips was in attendance but frankly he was just as astonished as the rest of the party goers, a little drunk off champagne and a few malt whiskeys too.

The security men frantically discussed ways in which they could detain Carruthers, neither of them with the clear thinking or foresight required for such a task at this moment in time, given the heavy breathing and adrenalin surge they were all experiencing. Fortunately, one of the braver guests who had made his way over, just itching to get involved in the action, volunteered an idea which may have just worked. As the guards wrestled him into position, the party goer tied Carruthers hands behind his back with his patterned neck tie.

Attention from the bulk of the crowd members who had remained in the vicinity, either through valour or sheer frozen fear, quickly turned to the two bodies that lay still on the floor. One was Tommy, the other was Jack. When the shot fired, Jack had instinctively dived towards Tommy to attempt to save him, banging his head on the floor as he fell.

Tommy came round and it took him a few seconds to realise what had happened. People were surrounding him, eyes staring down, hands over mouths, some asking if he was ok. He felt ok, just confused. Then he saw the glossy, scarlet blood on his hands. He checked his body for a wound, both with his hands and mind, desperately trying to locate a source of pain, but he couldn't seem to find one. *Surely adrenalin couldn't mask a bullet wound?* That's when he realised Jack was lying there motionless next to him, almost on top of him.

Tommy sat up as people hurried to his aid, attempting to help him up. Tommy shrugged them off. *Kirsten. Where was Kirsten?* That's when he saw her standing there looking straight at him, she seemed ok, frightened and terribly upset, but physically ok. Dorian had made his way over and placed his arm around her shoulder.

"I'm ok," he mouthed to Kirsten before she even had to ask, her face said it all; she was worried sick, her trembling hands covered her mouth. Tommy's attention returned to Jack, who hadn't moved yet.

Tommy rolled him over and saw the wound as he attempted to piece together what had happened in his mind – *Had Jack had taken the bullet for me*? There was blood, lots of it. A pool was forming under Jack's body; his grey suit had turned a deep crimson, black almost. Tommy throat was nearly closed, his mouth dry.

"Jack!" He shouted as he cradled his mentor, "Jack! Please Jack! Don't you dare die on me, not now!" Tommy was crying, he felt helpless. "Somebody call an ambulance!"

"There's one on the way," a bystander called, timidly.

"Jack! Come on, please wake up, stay with me." Tommy pleaded.

There was a flickering of Jack's eyes, they opened slightly. He looked up, saw Tommy and attempted to smile. He gestured towards Tommy to shush and calm down.

"Shhh! Tom, its ok," Jack's voice was weak, "You're a wonderful boy, you've made me a better person. I'm an old man; I've lived a good life. You're special Thomas, you're very special." Jack began to drift, his eyes rolling back in his head, drifting in and out of consciousness.

"Jack, no, don't go!" Tommy begged, squeezing Jack tighter in his embrace. Blood spread all over Tommy's clothes and hands now as he held him closely.

"Please forgive me, lad." Jack whispered as his eyes closed softly.

"I do! I do! Please, please Jack no!" Tommy screamed.

Jack's body flopped in his arms. Tommy felt his body turn heavy and saw the life drift away from him as his soul departed. Tommy had no idea whether any of that kind of stuff was real, he'd never been very spiritual – who could afford to be in his circumstances – but when he looked down on Jack's blood stained body, he felt like a part of him had gone too.

Kirsten broke away from Dorian and pushed her way past the bystanders that surrounded them. She dropped to her knees next to Tommy and flung her arms round him. They were both crying, as were several of those in the immediate vicinity.

At that point the ambulance crew bulldozed their way onto the scene, dropping their bags and began their routine, checking for life and weighing up whether CPR was a viable response. It wasn't.

The paramedic was a short man, athletic build with crew-cut grey hair, perhaps in his fifties. He checked all of Jack's vital signs. It was evident that the paramedic had a heavy heart as he pulled a blanket over Jack's face, shaking his head as a definitive sign that Jack's time was over, his last chapter written, his final bell rung. Tommy whelped and put his head in his hands.

The room was in chaos as Tommy got up to his feet, he felt in a strange and surreal trance. He noticed that the Police had arrived and were marching Carruthers off towards the exit. He wasn't prepared to go lightly; he wrestled all the way out with four police officers, screaming and shouting.

Before he was bundled through the fire exit, he bellowed insults and threats back into the room towards Tommy and his family – the chilling words echoed through the room, 'This is not over!'

A blonde haired police woman dropped the gun that Carruthers had used into an evidence bag and sealed it up, scribbling something on it with a thin black marker pen. Other officers were taking witness statements and attempting to calm the crowd down, with the help of hotel staff.

Tommy felt empty. This was supposed to be a victory, but it felt so much like a loss – a heavy loss. The loss he felt was that of one of his dearest friends, a mentor who he trusted as much, if not more, than any family he'd ever known and he couldn't help but shoulder the blame.

He attempted to walk, but stumbled. Kirsten caught him and waved over an ambulance crew member to give Tommy a look over. She put a towel around Tommy and, with the help of Kirsten and Dorian in tow, walked him over to a chair and sat him down.

The paramedic checked Tommy over, speaking to him calmly and clearly. Tommy struggled to focus his eyes as the paramedic talked to him. She had a soothing voice that eventually allowed Tommy to block out the madness around him and bring himself back down to earth. Kirsten gently rubbed the top of his back and attempted to appear brave, holding back even more tears. Her smudged mascara gave the game away though; Tommy could see she was as traumatised as he was.

Mr Turner made his way over to see Tommy and Kirsten. He looked awkward and sheepish, as most people would in this situation.

"Hello, you two," Mr Turner said, "how are you holding up?"

"I've been better, Sir." Tommy said with a slight smile. Given the circumstances, Tommy could have been excused for a more animated response, or better still just plainly ignoring his Headteacher, but he knew Mr Turner meant well so he offered kindness in his voice. Tommy thought about this side of his character for a quick second and attributed it to Jack, the man that had taught him how to be a man.

"Oh I don't doubt that, Thomas." Mr Turner said, offering a pat on Tommy's shoulder. "And you Miss Cole?"

Kirsten wiped away her tears and sniffled a little before responding, "I'm ok thanks, Sir."

A police detective in a brown corduroy jacket, navy blue shirt and loose tie approached the table where Tommy was sitting.

"Good evening," he said, "My name is Detective Inspector Kelvin Brightwell, I just have a few questions for you Mr Dawson, if you feel up to it? I won't take up much of your time; I know this has been a really difficult time for you."

Before Tommy could respond, Mr Turner interjected, "I will tell you anything you need to know about that horrific beast Jim Carruthers! I saw the video, I heard what he said, who he is and what he has done and I saw him pull out his gun and... well, we all know what happened to Mr Brookfield so its senseless stating the obvious."

"Thank you, Mr...?" The detective asked.

"Turner. Mr Turner, of Wellington High School." Mr Turner gushed. "These are two of my finest pupils here, Mr Dawson and Miss Cole. That despicable man has been inside my school gates! Masquerading as a man of sincerity, all the while he has been... Those poor children."

Mr Turner tailed off; the realisation of just what Jim Carruthers – or Smiler – had actually done to his pupils over the years must have suddenly resonated and it seemed to almost suffocate him. He looked vacant as the sense of responsibility for his pupils overwhelmed him, almost as though he had allowed this to happen. He was visibly angry, but showed huge vulnerability too.

Tommy recognised this and felt for his Headmaster. "It's ok Mr Turner, I'll take it from here, we'll be fine, please don't worry," he said, grabbing Kirsten by the hand and squeezing it, tighter than ever. Tommy was so grateful for Kirsten, tonight had certainly convinced him that it wasn't a school boy crush on his best friend that he had been feeling; it was love, the real kind.

"You had some questions, detective?" Tommy asked.

The detective proceeded to interview Tommy, as informally as he could. He scribbled in his notepad, documenting as much as possible of what Tommy told him. He was delicate and seemed mindful of the sensitivity surrounding the information and the ordeal that he had been through. The detective had tired but engaging eyes and Tommy noticed he made extra effort to listen, with firm eye contact as he nodded along accordingly. Tommy liked Detective Brightwell, he was exactly what he needed right now.

Once Tommy opened the flood gates of information, he couldn't seem to stop. He told Brightwell almost everything that he knew about Smiler and Jim Carruthers. As it happened, Brightwell had been leading the Smiler case on and off for a few years. He shared a few details, about how he was exhausted having chased far too many leads down far too many blind alleys, greeted by nothing but ghosts, hearsay and the odd arrest of a two-bit drug runner, charged with community service and a slap on the wrist. As it turned out, Detective Brightwell liked Tommy, he was exactly what he needed right now.

Tommy told him as much as he could, leaving a small but major part out – the stuff about his mum. He wasn't sure what he wanted to do with that information yet, whether he should even talk to his mum about it, let alone a Police detective. It lay heavy in the pit of his stomach, aching with every slight thought.

Tommy was grateful for Brightwell's sixth sense as he recognised when Tommy had zoned out a little and called a halt to his questioning. He said that he'd gotten enough information for one day and advised Tommy to get himself home and rest. He gave out his card to both Kirsten and Tommy and told them he'd be round to visit in a few days to tie up the last few bits of their statements. He also mentioned something about getting a copy of the video from Jack's gym, but fortunately Dorian stepped in and handled this request, shepherding Brightwell over towards his friend Steady Eddie.

Feeling exhausted, Tommy eased himself to his feet with the help of Kirsten. He needed to get out of this room; it felt as though it was closing in on him. He glanced at Kirsten; her streaming mascara, her teary eyes and her dishevelled hair and wondered what he'd done to deserve such an amazing and loyal friend, not to mention how stunning she'd looked this evening. He couldn't think of anyone better to have been side by side with in the trenches.

The pair of them exchanged a look of unity, relief and despair all rolled into one. It was the strangest feeling. He felt as though he was stuck in a helpless limbo, torn between the shock and pain of losing his friend and mentor moments ago and the intense affection he felt towards Kirsten, which still scorched inside of him.

"What do you say we get out of here?" Kirsten said softly.

"You took the words right out of my mouth," Tommy replied.

"There's a song there somewhere, isn't there?" she joked.

Tommy laughed, "Very good... You're getting better with that music knowledge of yours!"

He limped on; the muscles all over his body were tightening by the second, almost as though he had been beaten up; the fall to the floor must have had more of an impact than he first thought.

Before they reached the double doors of the King Louis suite, just about away from the mayhem, Kirsten stopped in her tracks and, keeping hold of his hand, turned Tommy to face her. She looked serious all of a sudden and her gaze was intense.

"Really, you think? Well, what's the next line of that song?" said Kirsten.

A more serious tone surfaced in her voice and Tommy detected nerves. He thought for a second and realised why.

"I think you know what the next line of the song is," Tommy said after a moment, reaching delicately for Kirsten's other hand and pulling her towards him ever so gently.

Their noses almost touched as he looked deep into her iridescent eyes, so deep that he could see the purity of her bare soul and it was as attractive as her exterior. He wiped away a remaining tear which skirted the top of her cheekbone and she returned the favour. Tommy could feel her breath on his face, the intimacy was heated and despite the atrocious circumstances which had occurred moments ago, he wanted so very desperately to kiss her soft, plump lips. He felt exposed, a vulnerability he'd never experienced before.

He couldn't figure out if their familiarity added more pressure to this situation, but he had suddenly found himself immersed in this quixotic daze, so didn't rightly care either way. Kirsten appeared to ready herself and, moistening her lips, she leaned forward slightly. Tommy felt an explosion of adrenalin surge around his body. *This is it.*

Out of nowhere came the booming voice of Mr Turner, "Goodnight Mr Dawson and Miss Cole!"

Tommy looked down and sighed, realising that yet again they had been interrupted at a crucial moment. He could help but smirk, questioning whether the universe was trying to tell him that this wasn't such a good idea. Their fleeting fire was instantly dampened and Kirsten offered a grin and a roll of the eyes that suggested she too was cursing the universe and its interfering agenda.

"Goodnight Mr and Mrs Turner," they both said simultaneously, an air of frivolity in their voices.

The moment had passed and Tommy felt unsure as to whether to force the situation and risk ruining it or it not living up to the expectation he had now built up in his head. *So close!* One thing he was sure of now though, was that Kirsten most definitely reciprocated the feelings he had towards her; he had just seen it in her eyes.

Whilst he was mulling these things over in his head, Kirsten took him by surprise, she grasped control of the situation and threw her arms around him, opting for the safer, but just as affectionate gesture of a friendly hug. She squeezed him tight and he felt everything he needed to feel right there in that moment. She kissed him softly on the cheek, making sure her lips lingered long enough for him to consider it more intimate than your average peck. She pulled her lips away and whispered gently in his ear, "I love you."

Tommy felt prickles all the way down his neck and spine, but Kirsten didn't hang around for a response. She handled it so coolly that he swooned for her even more. Tommy felt warmness inside of him that he'd never felt in his whole life. The problem was that it faded so quickly; as soon as he thought about Jack, Carruthers and his dad, it was joined subconsciously by an unpleasant feeling of guilt and despair.

The loss of Jack would no doubt weigh heavily on him for the remainder of his days; however he took slight consolation in the fact that it finally felt as though their quest was over.

Hand in hand, they headed towards the doors of the King Louie suite, leaving the carnage behind them. They could at least try and rest tonight and hopefully sleep with both eyes shut.

CHAPTER EIGHTEEN

"All rise!" The court clerk announced sternly, his words instantaneously shushing those in attendance.

Court Room 1 at Blackchester Crown Court was busy today. Day trippers had travelled from all over, a bulk of those from Granville-upon-sea, to see the outcome of the highly publicised trial of former councillor, Jim Carruthers, also known as drug king pin, Smiler.

The media had been all over the story since the showdown two months ago at the Whitmore Hotel and it had caught the attention of many folk who wanted to see the disgraceful and unforgivable crimes that had terrorised Granville for 30 years, punished accordingly. Although some argued that no punishment would ever be severe enough.

Tommy had tried to shy away from the media attention he had received, a mixture of wanting to get on with his life and a feeling of resentment towards the very same media who failed to report a single story or rumour about Carruthers and Smiler for decades.

Tommy sat in the court, feet tapping nervously, palms sweating. Kirsten sat next to him, putting on a brave and confident front but Tommy suspected she was equally as nervous. It was a grand old court room, furnished with rich mahogany seating, tables and benches, which rose in the style of an amphitheatre towards the back of the room. The public gallery was full, with spectators flocking to the balconies above to get a peek at the action.

This was it. Tommy was worried, but not nearly as worried as he was the days previously when he had to take the stand to be a material witness against his nemesis, his father's murderer. He felt like he'd done ok, despite Carruthers' highly paid, aristocratic barrister using all kinds of court room gamesmanship to try and trip him up. He'd tried to smear Tommy's reputation by dragging up his personal life and family circumstances, which made him uneasy and triggered an uncomfortable day.

Fortunately, no matter how much Carruthers' barrister earned, there were no tricks or loop holes that could get him out of the damning evidence that the prosecution presented, or so Tommy and his team hoped. He was being tried for the murder of Jack Brookfield as well as his Dad, Timothy Dawson. There were also charges of extortion, child sexual abuse, drug trafficking and distribution, just to name a few.

The Police had worked hard and managed to build a solid bank of evidence that they felt would put Carruthers away for a long time, with brave victims coming forward to appear as witnesses in the hope that they could contribute towards putting away the man who had tortured their minds, bodies and souls for too long, possibly offering them a small fraction of closure.

Amongst the brave witnesses was Rosie-Leigh Warrender, who described her horrendous experience as a victim of Carruthers' monstrous abuse 6 years prior. Rosie-Leigh was 20 years-old now and had been in and out of drug rehabilitation and mental health institutions up and down the country after dropping out of school at the age of 15. She recalled the day her innocence left her for good, stolen by the hands of the man standing in the dock and how he physically and sexually abused her for two years. She had never told a single person up until six weeks ago, when she heard about the witness appeal and walked apprehensively into Granville police station to give her statement.

There was also Harry Sullivan, a 35 year old man who was now married with two children. He worked for a charity supporting victims of domestic violence – a long way from the dark pit which he found himself in as a 14 year old boy, courtesy of Smiler. Mr Sullivan, with tears in his eyes, spoke of how he craved status as a teenager and Smiler tricked him into believing he could offer it him, failing to mention at the time of the horrific cost. Mr Sullivan described in detail how Carruthers would lure him to one of his many establishments, ply him with drink and drugs and take advantage of him, threatening him with exposure or death if he told anybody. He told the court how he followed Smiler because of the promise of status only to find pain, isolation, humiliation and torturous sadness. He also spoke of how moving away to live with his grandparents was his saviour, he managed to escape but he was aware and saddened by how many that didn't. Oddly, before stepping down from the witness stand, Mr Sullivan looked Carruthers straight in the eye and thanked him for making him the strong man, Father and husband he was today and attributed his empathetic skills within his profession to the experience of going to hell and back as a teenager. It was an extremely powerful moment in the case that condemned Carruthers even further.

Carruthers' defence had been manslaughter, claiming he hadn't meant to kill Jack Brookfield and that the other evidence was admissible based on the quality of the video and how it was obtained – plus the body of Timothy Dawson had still never been found. As for the abuse victims that had come forward, the defence treated them like roadkill, casting them aside, as if it was a ridiculous notion for a man of Carruthers' perceived stature to have committed such crimes. Tommy expected the defence to put up a fight, but they really laid it on thick, ridiculing these brave people, claiming were merely jumping on the bandwagon and attempting to smear the good name of Jim Carruthers in the hope of a compensation pay day.

The courtroom had been animated, with families and friends chomping at the bit to serve Carruthers their own version of justice, with one man being ordered away from court and barred, following his threats to kill Carruthers and feed him his own private parts.

Despite all of this, and being detained for the two months that had passed, Carruthers had appeared smartly dressed during the trial and composed. Today as he stood in the dock waiting to hear his fate, he wore a navy blue suit jacket, waistcoat and pants, with a crisp white shirt and gold tie. He was clearly still aiming for the slick, reliable councillor look, an attempt to cast doubt into the minds of those in attendance perhaps, but more importantly, the 12 jurors, who were now making their way back to the jury box.

Judge Michael Dennett shuffled to his bench and took his seat, a mahogany throne with royal green leather. He was an commanding man with a large frame, his black gown a little snug around the chest. The foreman for the jury took up his seat at the front left hand side of the bench and was asked to stand.

"Have the jury reached a verdict which at least ten of you agree upon?" Judge Dennett asked.

Everybody in the court room sat on the edge of their seats. The atmosphere was tense, like a scene from a court room thriller. Tommy's heart was in his mouth. He hadn't noticed, but Kirsten was squeezing his hand so tightly, his fingers had turned white.

"Yes, we have reached a unanimous verdict on all charges, your honour." The foreman responded. He was a short man who seemed to be taking his responsibility seriously. The paper he held in his hand trembled a little and his voice was a little pitchy.

The Judge made his way through the list of charges, each time asking the foreman how the jury found the defendant. Each time the foreman responded with the same answer.

"Guilty, your honour!" the foreman said after the final charge had been read out.

There were pockets of cheers within the crowd which were bitter sweet, given the crimes that had been discussed in great, sickening detail in the courtroom over the last week.

Carruthers' head sank in resignation, before the Judge gave his closing statement. It was the moment Tommy had been waiting for.

"Mr Carruthers," Judge Dennett began, "in all my years as a Judiciary, I can honestly say I have never encountered such vindictive, calculated and despicable crimes from a man who has totally and utterly abused his power and the trust placed in him by the people he was elected to protect, all the while destroying the lives of so many innocent children, adults and families and holding the town of Granville to ransom. Mr Carruthers I have no choice but to sentence you to a Whole-life Order. At your age, this means you will draw your last breath inside the walls of prison and never be considered for parole. Guards, take him away."

"You little bastard!" Carruthers screamed over at Tommy, his composure shot as he now had nothing to lose. "I'm going to kill you!"

He tried to leap over the dock but was quickly restrained and dragged off towards the steps which led down to the cells underneath the court. Tommy instinctively put his hand across Kirsten as if to protect her, not that maniac would have got anywhere near them, there were enough guards to manage a rival football match.

Tommy stared dead pan towards Carruthers. He showed no emotion. He didn't even know what emotion he was feeling right now. Kirsten grasped his hand softly; as usual she was right on cue with her sign of solidarity and affection.

Carruthers' screaming disappeared into the depths of the Crown Court building. The spectators began to get up and leave, gossiping and smiling, pleased that justice had been served. One man tapped Tommy on the shoulder in support; another lady suggested a prison cell was too good for Carruthers and that she'd have strung him up by his bits and left him to rot.

"Come on Tommy; let's get out of here... It's over." Kirsten said with a wry smile.

He hoped that now the case was over, he might be able to find the time to talk about those feelings they had for each other. Over the last few months it just hadn't felt quite right. He had been worrying that he should be more concerned about the case, the loss of Jack and the truth about his mother and father – which he was, but he couldn't help but lose focus of that from time to time, falling for Kirsten further and further. Whenever they spent time together his stomach was in knots, yearning to tell her how he felt.

Kirsten had been so supportive and respectful of what he was going through and, whilst he detected – and enjoyed – the occasional instances of flirting, he felt as though she didn't push the issue any more than it needed to be and he appreciated that. He cherished those words that she whispered in his ear in the Whitmore hotel, they still floated around his head as though she'd just said them. He longed now for the opportunity to say the same three words back to her but realised he'd have to wait just a little while longer, perhaps he'd ask to take her out on an official date, or something like that.

The pair of them got up and walked out of the court room.

"When we get back to Granville, do you want to come to my mum's house for dinner? She'd love to see you." Kirsten asked.

Tommy smiled, "I'd love to, but there's somewhere I need to go first."

Tommy walked through the door of 10 Frampton Road, the home he'd longed to escape for so long had become the place he wanted to be more than anywhere. His mum and Derek were sat on the couch awaiting his return. The radio was on quietly in the background.

"Well?" Derek jumped up and exclaimed before Tommy had even shut the door behind him.

"He got a life sentence, a full life sentence, no parole." Tommy said. He offered a smile but it was blatant he was a little underwhelmed.

"That's the best we could have hoped for though, right?" Derek said, attempting to rally the troops and celebrate the victory, however small it seemed in comparison to what they had lost.

"Yeah, I suppose." Tommy said putting an arm around Derek's shoulder and squeezing it slightly. "Derek, do you mind if I have a quiet word with Mum?"

Derek looked at their mum, then back at Tommy. "Of course not bro, go right ahead, I'm off to the shop anyway, I'll pick us up some celebratory beers... catch you later!" Derek tapped Tommy on the back, before heading out the door.

Tommy moved over towards the couch and sat down next to his mum. She wore a baggy woollen sweater which hid her painfully thin frame. He reached out and grabbed her hands and held them in his. His mum looked a little uncomfortable with this demonstration of intimacy, but she went with it.

"I'm so proud of you, Thomas" she said, tears filling her eyes. Tommy couldn't recall his mum ever saying those words to him. His stomach did a little somersault.

"Mum, nothing – I mean nothing – will ever be enough to punish that man for what he did," Tommy said, his words were strong and emotional as his eyes too began to fill up too. "I'm so sorry."

His mum, a little confused and taken aback, had the option of playing it safe in assuming that Tommy was referring to Carruthers murdering his father. He wasn't of course. He was referring to what Carruthers had put her through as a young girl, a turn of events that had changed her life forever and still controlled her every move. Tommy's double entendre was intentional, he hoped it might allow her to realise that he did in fact know the secret of her troubled past, but with the safety net of it still being left unsaid, just in case this was something she wasn't ready to address with him yet, if at all.

"Tommy, listen, you have nothing to be sorry for, in fact, it's me that should be sorry. Regardless of what we have been through as a family, I simply have not been there for you in the way that I should have."

Tommy squeezed his mum's hand tighter, he didn't tell her not to worry about it or that she was wrong, because she was right. These were the words he had longed to hear his whole life.

"It's ok, Mum, we've got by." Tommy said.

"I've been a shit Mother Tommy, let's be honest!" his mum sniggered; she was embarrassed and vulnerable, snot ballooning from her nose. She wiped the snot away with a tissue. "But that is going to change, I promise. I've spoken to my drug worker, for real this time, not just as a means to get a script or my benefits. I'm going clean. We've looked at a residential detox followed by supported community rehabilitation. It'll mean me going away for a while, but we all know you're capable of looking after yourself!"

Tommy was astounded and so proud. He was stuck for words so he threw his arms around his mum. The embrace was warm, despite his mum's fragility. Maybe there was love there after all. It was the first time Tommy had ever heard his mum talk so openly and rationally about their situation. It was clear that the imprisonment of Carruthers earlier today had given his mum the confidence and bravery to escape the solitude she had been torturing herself within all these years and make a change for the better. Tommy felt like this was the first step towards the rest of their lives.

Suddenly a breaking news alert came on the radio and the reporter seemed lively, the kind of excitement that a big news story brought to a journalist. Tommy leaned over and turned the volume dial up a couple of notches as he and his Mum listened intently.

"Police were called to an incident just outside Blackchester earlier today after an armoured prison vehicle was ambushed by a gang of armed men wearing masks. It is believed the attack was an attempt to break out notorious criminal, Jim Carruthers, who was sentenced to life imprisonment today at Blackchester Crown Court. Reports coming in are suggesting that three members of the prison service who were transporting Mr Carruthers, otherwise known as drug king pin, Smiler, were shot dead. The gang escaped without trace, with no sign of Jim Carruthers."

LOOK OUT

FOR THE SECOND BOOK IN

THE GRANVILLE SERIES

"THE CHEMIST"

AUTUMN 2019

ABOUT THE AUTHOR

Nathan Parker is a professional, working in the field of children and young people, with various experiences within youth work, substance misuse and mental health, spanning over 10 years.

Writing is currently a hobby, as Nathan works full-time on his mission to make his home town the best possible place it can be for young people to grow up in.

His writing style incorporates real life challenges and adversity into gripping and mysterious plots.

Printed in Great Britain
by Amazon

56795523R00154